THE
DISAPPEARING
STRANGER

THE
DISAPPEARING
STRANGER

Lois Walfrid Johnson

BETHANY HOUSE PUBLISHERS
MINNEAPOLIS, MINNESOTA 55438

Except for historic characters—Big Gust, Trader Carlson, and A. Hult—the characters in this book are fictitious. Any resemblance to persons living or dead is coincidental.

Published by Bethany House Publishers
A Ministry of Bethany Fellowship, Inc.
6820 Auto Club Road, Minneapolis, Minnesota 55438

Printed in the United States of America

Library of Congress Cataloging-in-Publication Data

Johnson, Lois Walfrid.
    The disappearing stranger / Lois W. Johnson.
      p. cm. — (The Adventures of the northwoods ; bk. 1)
    Summary: When her mother marries Mr. Nordstrom, Kate moves to a farm in northwest Wisconsin, solves a mystery, and learns to adjust to her new stepfamily.

    [1. Swedish Americans—Fiction. 2. Stepfamilies—Fiction. 3. Mystery and detective stories. 4. Christian life—Fiction.]
I. Title. II. Series: Johnson, Lois Walfrid. Adventures of the northwoods ; bk. 1.
PZ7.J63255Di 1990
[Fic]—dc20   90–2
ISBN 1–55661–100–5   CIP
                                           AC

To Marie Johnson, the Mama in the picture,
and to Mom and Dad Walfrid,
for telling me the way it was.

LOIS WALFRID JOHNSON is the bestselling author of more than twenty books. These include *You're Worth More Than You Think!* and other Gold Medallion winners in the LET'S-TALK-ABOUT-IT STORIES FOR KIDS series about making choices. Novels in the ADVENTURES OF THE NORTHWOODS series have received awards from Excellence in Media, the Wisconsin State Historical Society, and the Council for Wisconsin Writers.

Lois has a great interest in historical mystery novels, as you may be able to tell! She and her husband, Roy, a former widower, are the parents of a blended family and live in rural Wisconsin.

Preface

Yes, there really was a train called the Blueberry Special. In the early 1900's it chugged its way into northwest Wisconsin, then turned around on the same track.

So, too, was there a man of great strength—a seven-foot, six-inch tall village marshal named Big Gust. Loved by law-abiding citizens, he quickly dealt with troublemakers in the small town of Grantsburg.

Near the shores of Spirit Lake, the one-room country school still stands, though children no longer come there for learnin'. Through the pages of this book you may hear the sound of their laughter.

If you had lived in that time you could have known people like Kate and Anders, Mama and Papa, Lars and Tina. You could have known Lutfisk, their dog, and visited Windy Hill, their farm on the edge of the big woods.

It's not too late. Even now, you can join Kate and Anders in the adventure of *The Disappearing Stranger*.

The Riverboat Adventures

Adventures of the Northwoods

9610

Contents

1

Kate's Secret Plan

*O*n the way home from school Katherine O'Connell slowed her steps. Around her, the noises of Minneapolis filled the street. A horse trotted past, clip-clopping on the cobblestones. Circling a mound of snow, Kate found a place to stop.

The black hair that escaped her braid curled around her face. In the afternoon sunlight her deep blue eyes sparkled. The air felt warm for a Minnesota winter, but twelve-year-old Kate barely noticed. She had an idea.

Rolling it around in her mind, she considered the idea from this way and that. More than once she had tumbled headlong into a plan, sometimes with surprising results. Yet this one might work.

At last Kate tossed her head. Flipping her long braid over her shoulder, she made up her mind.

Walking quickly, she plunged down the street. The church was only a block away. A year ago she wouldn't have thought of going there for help. But that was before Daddy died.

Even now, Kate felt surprised by her idea. Yet it was a good one. She felt sure of that.

At the bottom of the church steps she paused, suddenly

afraid. From here Kate could barely see the tall steeple reaching
to the sky. Across the street a grocery wagon stopped, and a boy
climbed down. Lifting a wooden box filled with food, he carried
it into a house.

Seeing him there, Kate knew it was time to be home. Mama
would wonder where she was.

Turning, Kate hurried up the wide stone steps. As she pulled
open the heavy door, she tried to look like the young lady Mama
wanted her to be. Somehow Kate always forgot.

Inside, where the sunlight did not reach, the entryway
seemed dim and cold. Quickly Kate opened another door.

In the main part of the church, afternoon sunlight brightened
the large windows. Pews stretched away to the front. Kate stood
there a moment, thinking about Mama. Last night she had cried
in the dark again.

When Kate asked, "Are you all right?" Mama sniffled her yes.

"Are you lonesome for Daddy?" Kate asked next.

Mama's answer sounded clearer, as though she'd pulled the
quilt away from her head. "Yes, Kate. Go back to sleep."

But Kate had one more question. "Mama, do you ever get
lonesome for Sweden?"

At the age of seventeen Mama had come from Sweden by
herself. "Sometimes," she answered, her voice soft. "Sometimes."

Mama's words scared Kate. *What if she decides to go back to
Sweden? I'd have to leave all my friends—Sarah Livingston and
Michael Reilly—*

Often the children teased Michael, saying, "You're sweet on
Kate!" Michael always turned red, but he never denied it.

In the darkness of night Kate lay there a long time before
going back to sleep, wondering, *What can I do?*

Now Kate started down the side aisle of the church. As she
passed the organ, she stopped and looked back. "Do I dare?"
she asked herself, then felt surprised she'd spoken aloud.

As she looked around, the church seemed empty.

Moving quickly, Kate turned back to the pipe organ. Again
she glanced around. "No one will know," she muttered. Without
a sound Kate slid onto the bench.

For a long time she'd wanted to sit there, feeling the ivory keys beneath her fingers. For what seemed forever she'd wanted to make the wonderful big sounds the organist played every Sunday. Whenever the sermon seemed long, Kate thought about the sound of the music.

She knew the organ wouldn't work without someone hand pumping the bellows that brought in air. Yet she touched the keys the way the organist did, pretending she knew how to play. *I could be a great organist. I could travel around America putting on concerts. If only I could learn.*

Then from somewhere in the dimly lit corners came a sound. In a second Kate was off the bench, starting down the aisle once more.

At the front of the church, she reached a hallway, then a large door. Kate straightened her shoulders, hoping she looked taller. Before she could change her mind, she raised her hand and knocked.

As the sound echoed in the stillness, Kate wished she hadn't come. In all her twelve years she'd never been so scared. Except when Daddy died, that is.

Maybe Pastor Munson won't be here. Kate felt torn between wanting to see him and fearing what he'd think. Just as she turned to run, the door opened.

"Kate!" exclaimed the pastor. *"God dag!"*

His words sounded like "Good dog," and Kate knew only a few words of Swedish. Because Daddy was Irish and Mama Swedish, Kate spoke English at home. Yet she knew Pastor Munson was saying, "Good day," and managed to squeak out her hello.

Whenever Pastor Munson stood in the front of the church, he looked tall and stern. Now as Kate sat down, he seemed still more frightening.

"What can I do for you?" he asked from his big chair behind the big desk.

Kate's hands tightened, and she found herself bunching her skirt inside nervous fingers. *I wish I'd never come. Where do I begin?*

In the silence someone knocked on the door. "Excuse me,"

said Pastor Munson. "I'll be right back."

As he went into the hallway, Kate looked around for a way of escape. Books lined two walls of the study. On the third wall hung a large calendar. JANUARY, 1906. Nearby, the sun streamed through a window.

Seeing the sunlight, Kate felt better. When Pastor Munson returned, she knew what to say.

This time he smiled as he asked, "Can I help you with something?"

Kate swallowed. "When you preached Sunday—" She stopped, afraid to go on. For a moment she waited, but he waited too.

"Yah?" It was the Swedish yes, and his voice sounded encouraging. Yet Kate's hand shook as she reached up and touched the small locket on a chain around her neck. She thought of Daddy and how he'd given her the locket on her last birthday before he died.

Remembering Daddy gave Kate courage. Her voice steadied. "In church on Sunday you said we could talk to you when we have a problem."

Pastor Munson nodded, and Kate went on. "Well, I have a problem. Or rather, Mama has a problem."

"Yah?" asked Pastor Munson again.

Kate had to go on. "Mama needs a husband."

Pastor Munson cleared his throat. "Oh, indeed?"

Now Kate's words came in a rush. "She's always tired. She works hard sewing dresses for rich ladies. And she's been sick, off and on all fall."

Kate stopped, and Pastor Munson nodded, "Yah." This time the word wasn't a question.

"But I think it's more. Since Daddy died she's been so—"

Pastor Munson finished for her. "Hopeless."

"All of Mama's family lives in Sweden." For a moment Kate was silent, looking at her hands as they twisted in her lap. Then she tried again. "Sometimes when I wake up at night Mama's crying. In the morning she pretends she's all right. But her eyes—"

"Look sad."

"Yah," said Kate, surprised she'd used the Swedish yes.

Whenever she heard Mama crying, Kate longed to be a family again. To have Daddy back, telling his funny stories. To sing together and laugh. Even to herself, Kate couldn't quite explain it. But to love each other.

She tried to put the thought away. Daddy couldn't come back, not ever.

Kate felt relieved that Pastor Munson seemed to understand about Mama. Somehow he didn't seem quite so stern. In fact, his eyes looked kind. When he smiled, she knew he wasn't making fun of her, the way boys at school might do.

"What's it been? A year now since your papa died in that construction accident?"

Kate nodded. Daddy had been strong, as though nothing would ever happen to him. He'd been a good carpenter. When he came home from work, he always swung her off the floor with a big hug. Sometimes he danced around the kitchen, doing an Irish jig. Tears came into Kate's eyes just thinking about it.

A slow smile spread across Pastor Munson's face. "I think you're right. Your mama needs a husband."

"You do?"

"Yah, surely. But I have a question. Do you feel ready to have a new papa?"

Suddenly Kate felt afraid. She hadn't thought about that.

"It would change your life, you know. A new papa might have a family of his own."

"Maybe I'd get a sister," Kate answered. "I've always wanted a little sister. But what if I got a *brother*? That would be *awful*." To herself she added, *Unless it was someone like Michael, that is.*

For a moment she sat there, biting her lip and thinking. *Pastor Munson will find a husband from Minneapolis. I can still see my friends. I can learn to play the organ.*

Then she remembered Mama crying at night. More than anything, she wanted Mama happy again.

In that moment Kate made up her mind. Inside, she felt uneasy, as though something wasn't quite right. Yet she pushed the feeling away. When she answered, her voice was clear and strong. "I want Mama to have a new husband."

"Then I'll pray," answered Pastor Munson.

"And you'll help?"

"If I can."

"You won't tell Mama I've been here?"

Pastor Munson shook his head, his face solemn. "It'll be our secret."

"Good." Kate felt relieved. She stood up to go. "It's all settled then."

But Pastor Munson held up his hand. "Just a minute, young lady."

Kate stopped in her flight to the door.

"Before you go, we need to pray about it. We better ask God to help us."

Kate nodded. "I thought you'd be good at that."

"Oh, I am. I've had lots of practice." His dark eyes twinkled. "But since you asked my help, I thought you'd like to pray for me."

"Me? *I* pray for *you*?"

"Yah." The word was soft. Then the room was silent, filled with waiting.

"Me?" Kate asked again. Even when she had felt the most scared, she hadn't thought of anything that awful. "But that's what pastors are paid for."

Pastor Munson's eyes seemed to smile, yet his voice sounded serious. "It's hard being a matchmaker. I think I need God's help."

Slowly Kate sat down again. Slowly she bowed her head. Her thoughts felt like the squirrels racing up and down the tree outside the church. *What do I say?* she wondered in panic. *Me pray for him?*

"Just make it simple," said Pastor Munson as though reading her thoughts.

That made Kate even more uncomfortable. In the silence a clock ticked, and the moment stretched long between them. Kate's ideas refused to come out in order. For a long time she'd been angry at God. Often she'd told him, "If you love me, God, why did you let Daddy die?" For a long time she'd told herself,

"God can't possibly hear my prayer."

But Kate felt desperate. For Mama's sake she needed to try. And Pastor Munson waited.

Kate squeezed her eyes shut and cleared her throat. "Mama needs your help, God," she prayed. "She needs a husband. Help Pastor Munson find one. Ah-men."

As Kate looked up, Pastor Munson opened his eyes. A wide smile lit his face. Standing up, he reached out his hand to shake Kate's. "Thank you. I'll do the best I can."

Somehow Kate felt better. Mumbling a quick thanks, she headed for the door. As she reached the safety of the hallway, she even felt good about what she'd done.

She turned back to Pastor Munson. "I can hardly wait to see what happens!"

2

Sunday Surprise

Outside, Kate ran the entire two blocks to where she and Mama rented rooms on the second floor of a large house. Bounding up the steps, Kate flung open the kitchen door. A man stood just inside—a heavyset man with his back toward Kate.

Even without seeing his face, she knew who it was—the landlord, asking for his rent. A shiver slid down Kate's spine, a shiver not caused by the January cold.

"I won't force you out in the middle of winter," he was saying. He drew himself up to his full height. "After all, I'm a just man. But mark my words, by March 15 for sure."

Stepping around Kate, he headed down the stairs.

Mama stood by the wood cookstove. In the lamplight her hair looked golden. It was drawn up, piled on top of her head. Quiet tears wet her cheeks.

Kate walked into her mother's arms, and Mama hugged her. "It's all right, Kate. It's all right."

But Kate felt sure that it wasn't. Stepping back, she looked up into Mama's face. Kate knew her own eyes were a deeper blue than Mama's. Mama also was tall for a woman, and Kate was short for her age. Now Kate cried out in protest, "I hate him! I hate him!"

Mama's stern voice interrupted. "Stop it, Kate!" She turned
to the cookstove and stirred the watery stew. When she spoke
again, her voice sounded tired. "He's only asking for what is his.
If I could just earn more money, we'd keep up."

Kate stalked out of the kitchen, her hands over her ears. She
knew it was true, but didn't want to hear the hopelessness in
Mama's words. Sometimes Mama sewed far into the night. Other
times it was hard to find work.

"Is there anything else we can sell?" asked Kate, looking
around.

Mama followed her into the sitting room, her shoulders
slumped with discouragement.

"I'll find more work," Kate said, her voice angry. "I'll drop
out of school."

"No!" exclaimed Mama. "You're working enough after school
and Saturdays. You need book learning to make your way."

"Dumb old Mr. Mark-My-Words!" Kate muttered, then bit
her lip. She didn't want to argue with Mama. They'd talked
about all this before. But the pain inside Kate went deep.

For two long weeks she woke up every morning, hoping
she'd hear about a husband for Mama. "The rest of January, then
February," Kate told her one morning. "Fifteen days in March,
and he'll make us leave. Where will we go?"

Mama didn't answer, but a new line creased her forehead.

As Kate waited and wondered, the snowy days stretched out
forever. *Maybe Pastor Munson forgot his promise. Maybe it's too
big an order, even for God.*

Then one Saturday in the middle of January Mama sold another piece of furniture. Coming home, she said, "Help me,
Kate. Let's move my trunk into the dining room."

Kate grabbed hold of the leather handle on one end. Mama
took the handle on the opposite side. Together they slid the trunk
across the floor of their small sitting room. A curl tumbled onto
Mama's forehead, making her look young and helpless.

But Kate knew that Mama was not helpless. Kate knew the
story of the wooden trunk and wanted to hear it again. "It came
all the way from Sweden?"

"Yah," said Mama. "I had the America fever. All over Sweden

people left. I just had to go to America!"

"And your papa built this trunk?" Kate asked the way she had since she was little.

Mama nodded. "I worked on a farm as a hired girl. I saved everything I earned for a ticket to America. Finally when I was seventeen, my papa—your grandpapa—threw up his hands. 'All right, all right! It's useless trying to keep you here!' He started building the trunk.

"When it was time for me to leave, Mama didn't want to go to the train. She said, 'I just can't manage it.' So Papa and I went. It was the only time I ever saw him cry."

"And when you got to America you worked as a maid?" prodded Kate, the way she always did.

"In a boardinghouse," Mama answered. "I saved my money. I had my picture taken and sent it home to Mama and Papa."

Letting go of the trunk handle, Mama went into the bedroom. She returned with a framed picture. "That's when they had *this* taken."

Mama's finger pointed. "Mama and Papa sitting in the middle. My five sisters and two brothers around them. And that's Sophia—the sister closest in age. She's holding *my* picture."

"So you could still be part of the family," said Kate, hoping Mama would go on.

But for once Mama didn't tell the rest of the story. Putting down the picture, she took the trunk handle again. "Over here," she said, giving a mighty tug. "Next to the kitchen door."

When the trunk was in place, Mama set the picture on its wide, flat top. Then Kate knew why Mama wanted to move the trunk. When she started supper, Mama looked through the doorway at the picture. She looked that way often.

The sadness in Mama's large blue eyes made Kate uneasy. *What if she decides to go back to Sweden?* Kate wondered more than once.

At the same time, there was something about the picture that drew Kate. Deep inside she ached with wanting to be part of a big family. *Will Mama and I ever be really happy again?*

The next morning Kate was still thinking about the picture when she and Mama set out for Sunday services. Inside the church, Mama headed for the pew where she knew Kate liked to sit. From there Kate could watch the organist. Listening to the big sounds, she forgot her worry about Mama. During the sermon she let the songs play over and over in her mind. At last she felt sure she remembered every note.

As the sermon dragged on, Kate thought about Jenny Lind. People called her the Swedish nightingale because of the way she sang. Long before Kate was born, Miss Lind toured the United States, giving concerts and hope.

If I could play the organ, I'd make people feel that way. Even Mama would feel better. She'd laugh the way she used to when Papa sang. As though it were yesterday, Kate remembered Papa's Irish tenor voice.

When Pastor Munson shook their hands after church, he pulled Kate and Mama aside. "Mrs. Munson has a fine chicken today. Will you join us for dinner?"

The pastor and his wife lived next to the church. When Kate and Mama entered the parlor, they discovered someone already there. Pastor Munson introduced him. "This is Carl Nordstrom. He visited our church today."

As Mama and Mr. Nordstrom said their *"God dag's,"* Kate looked quickly at Pastor Munson. His face was as solemn as ever, but a smile tugged at the corners of his mouth. Just in time Kate swallowed a giggle. He hadn't forgotten his promise!

During the meal, Kate looked at Mr. Nordstrom whenever she could. His black suit coat covered wide, strong shoulders, and Kate guessed he must be well over six feet tall. His brown hair and moustache and beard were neatly trimmed. His skin looked like Daddy's from working outside.

Kate liked Mr. Nordstrom. Maybe he'd make a good husband for Mama.

As they ate chicken and mashed potatoes and gravy, Pastor Munson asked Mr. Nordstrom about his family. "Tina is four, Lars almost nine, and Anders twelve," he answered in an accent like Mama's. Now and then he used Swedish words, but his English was good.

A little sister! Kate wanted to know more. *I've always wanted a younger sister. But two brothers? Sarah says that brothers are terrible pests.*

"So, you know my old friend, Rev. Hult?" asked Pastor Munson.

Mr. Nordstrom nodded. "He's my pastor in Trade Lake. He said to give you greetings when I came to Minneapolis."

"Trade Lake?" asked Kate. She knew only grownups were supposed to speak, but she couldn't help it.

"Trade Lake, Wisconsin," answered Mr. Nordstrom. "It's the town closest to my farm. Trader Carlson has a big store there. Indians from miles around bring their furs to him."

"Oh," said Kate, her voice small. "You live in Wisconsin?" Her mind filled with the horror of it. *Wisconsin would be even worse than Sweden! Sarah says Wisconsin is a wilderness.*

Mr. Nordstrom nodded. "Yah, I'm a farmer."

"And your farm is in the big woods of Wisconsin?" Mama asked.

"On the edge of a big woods," said Mr. Nordstrom. "And on the edge of a steep hill. Windy Hill Farm, we call it."

His voice warmed with enthusiasm. "In the west we see sunsets over Rice Lake. South of the house I've cleared a field for corn, and north of the barn I'm clearing another. It's a good place to live."

But Kate wasn't impressed. "Do you have bears?" she asked, the horror within her growing. Flipping her long braid over her shoulder, she leaned forward. "My friend Sarah says there are big bears in Wisconsin."

Mr. Nordstrom smiled. "Yah, we have bears, sometimes five-hundred-pound ones. But they're more afraid of us than we need to be of them."

Kate didn't believe him. "But Sarah says bears are wild and mean and knock down log cabins, and break open bee hives, and—"

"Kate," Mama's voice was soft, but with a warning running through it. It was her reminder that children should be seen and not heard.

By now Kate had changed her mind. She didn't like the idea of Mr. Nordstrom from Wisconsin. She wished he'd go home and stay there.

"Mostly we have big Swedes," Mr. Nordstrom went on. "In

Grantsburg, where the train comes in, the village marshal is seven and a half feet tall and three hundred sixty pounds. He takes good care of any troublemakers!"

"Seven and a half feet?" Kate forgot to be quiet. She couldn't imagine someone that tall. Then she wondered about something else. "What kind of troublemakers do you have in Wisconsin?"

But Mama had questions of her own. "And your wife? How does she like living in the wilderness?"

Suddenly Kate felt scared, wishing Mama wouldn't ask. Now she'd find out.

Quickly Kate looked at Pastor Munson. Once more, a smile played around the corners of his mouth. Kate wished she could run away and hide.

Mr. Nordstrom turned to Mama, his eyes steady. "My wife died eight months ago. She had scarlet fever."

"I'm sorry," said Mama simply. "My husband died too—in a construction accident."

For a moment they looked at each other, Mr. Nordstrom's blue eyes meeting Mama's even bluer ones.

Again Kate felt scared. *This isn't the way it's supposed to be!* She wished Mama wouldn't look so beautiful. *She's supposed to get a husband from Minneapolis. She's supposed to stay right here.*

When it was time to say thanks for the meal, Mr. Nordstrom walked Kate and Mama home. Kate walked fast, wishing they wouldn't talk so much.

She liked seeing the light back in Mama's eyes. She liked hearing Mama laugh again. But she didn't like anything else about Mr. Nordstrom's visit.

That awful, nervous feeling in Kate's stomach wouldn't go away. What if Mama decided to marry Mr. Nordstrom? What if he asked them to move to the wilderness of Wisconsin? Kate couldn't think of anything worse.

3

Mama's Choice

*A*fter that, letters came from Wisconsin much too often for Kate's way of thinking. Each time a new one arrived, she felt more afraid. Mama's blue eyes sparkled all the time now. Often she asked, "Is there mail for me?"

One afternoon in February Mr. Nordstrom came to visit. When he left, Mama told Kate that in a month she and Mr. Nordstrom would get married.

"But do you love him?" asked Kate, suddenly forgetting about the rent they couldn't pay and how Mama used to cry during the night. "Do you love him the way you loved Daddy?"

"Not yet," answered Mama calmly. "But I will."

"You *will?*"

"I loved your Daddy very much." Mama's voice was warm with remembering. "He'll always have a special place in my life. Nothing can change that."

"But, Mama—" Kate interrupted.

Mama acted as though she hadn't heard. "Once your daddy and I talked. We talked about what I'd do if something happened to him." Suddenly Mama's eyes filled with tears.

She wiped them away and struggled to speak. "I didn't want to think about it. I didn't want anything to touch our love. But death did."

Mama swallowed, then went on. "On that day your daddy told me—"

"You'd have to go on," Kate finished the sentence. "You'd have to face things, even though you're afraid."

Mama smiled, a gentle smile that reached her eyes. "How did you know?"

In that moment Kate felt very grown up. "Once he said the same thing to me."

Mama opened her arms. Her hug felt good. When she spoke again, her words were muffled in Kate's hair. "I've prayed, and I believe Mr. Nordstrom is God's answer to help us. He's a good man, a kind man, a Christian. He'll take care of us. And I can help him."

"You'd marry him without *love*?" Kate was so startled she moved away from Mama's hug. "The kind of love you had for Daddy?" When she and Pastor Munson prayed, Kate thought Mama would wear a beautiful new dress and her eyes would shine with happiness.

Right now Mama's eyes were shiny with tears, but her voice was strong. "As we work together, I'll grow to love him. God's given me peace."

"God!" Kate wanted to spit out. Just in time she caught herself. She didn't dare tell Mama what she thought about God. Or about Pastor Munson for writing to Wisconsin for a husband. Mama could be stubborn, as stubborn as Kate.

"Aren't you afraid of living in a wilderness?" Kate asked, instead of what she wanted to say. "There'll be all kinds of scary, strange things."

Mama didn't answer, and Kate went on. "I'd like a little sister and a happy family. But two *brothers*? And one of them my age?"

Still Mama was silent.

Kate's voice rose. "I'd have to leave all my friends!"

"Yah," Mama answered, and Kate felt surprised. When Daddy was alive, she always said the English yes.

"Yah," Mama said again. "I'm sorry about that. But instead you'll have a family. And you'll make new friends."

"New friends in a wilderness? Sarah says we'd live in a log cabin. She says it's uncivilized, that wild animals run all over the place. We'd be out in the middle of nowhere!"

"Kate, wait and see," said Mama.

"I can't take organ lessons in a wilderness!"

A shadow crossed Mama's face. She sighed. "I know, Kate. But wait and see. Maybe it won't be as bad as you think."

"Wait and see? This is my *life!*" Kate's voice ended on a wail. She felt angry about the way God answered her prayer. Even more, she felt scared. Scared because Mama had accepted Mr. Nordstrom's offer of marriage. Scared about leaving Sarah and Michael and her other friends. Scared about the way her world was going to change.

Flipping her braid over her shoulder, Kate stood as tall as she could. "If I'd known this would happen, I never would have talked to Pastor Munson about you!"

"You *what*?" Mama's blue eyes were dark with anger. "*You* talked to Pastor Munson about *me*?"

"Oh!" Kate clapped her hand over her mouth. But it was too late.

"Just exactly what did you say, Katherine Marie O'Connell?"

Mama waited until the story came out. When Kate finished, two bright red spots flushed Mama's cheeks. Kate had never seen her so angry.

"Well, if that's the matter of it," Mama said, "I certainly will not see Mr. Carl Nordstrom from Wisconsin again. Never again. If he thinks I'm out looking for a husband—"

As the tears welled up in Mama's eyes, she whirled and stomped into the bedroom. Never before had Kate heard Mama slam a door. The sound echoed through their upstairs rooms.

Kate sank down on the floor and buried her face in her hands. It was just what she wanted. Yet it was so awful hurting Mama, so awful taking the happiness out of her eyes.

Then Kate remembered Mr. Mark-My-Words and the rent they weren't able to pay. March 15 was only a month away.

Kate felt scared again—more scared than she'd ever felt about living in a wilderness.

I can't even dream of a family anymore. Maybe living in Wisconsin wouldn't have been so bad after all.

———

In the two weeks that followed, Kate saw at least five letters addressed to Mrs. Ingrid O'Connell. Mama didn't answer one of them.

"Good!" Kate told herself. "We won't have to move to Wisconsin!" Yet the idea didn't please her the way it once would. As the days passed with Mama pretending nothing had happened, Kate felt ashamed. She felt even worse when she woke up to Mama crying at night.

Then one Friday evening, Kate heard a knock on the door. Opening it, she found Mr. Nordstrom on the steps. Under a long coonskin coat, he wore his black suit. His moustache and beard were trimmed close to his sun-weathered face.

" 'Evening, Kate," he said, tipping his hat. "I'd like to see your mama."

Kate backed away from the door. "What do you want?" she blurted out. "Train tickets cost money. It must be serious."

A strange look crossed Mr. Nordstrom's face. Kate felt embarrassed at being so forward. Then she remembered her manners. "Mama's here. Please come in."

In the sitting room, Mama put down her sewing and stood up. She did not look pleased. "Good evening, Mr. Nordstrom," she said, her voice stiff and formal. Yet as she hung up his coat, a soft pink flushed her cheeks.

When Mama sat down again, Mr. Nordstrom pulled up a chair opposite her. He looked even more uncomfortable than Mama. Twice he cleared his throat, but no words came.

Kate could hardly wait to hear what they'd say. Yet as she started to sit down, Mama turned to her.

"Thank you, Kate." That was Mama's way of telling her to leave.

Dragging her feet, Kate headed for the bedroom. Once inside, she left the door open a crack, then slid down to the floor, peeking through. Both Mama and Mr. Nordstrom sat exactly where they needed to be for Kate to see.

Mama's face looked frozen, as though she were the one who'd come in from the February night. "You must have had a cold trip, Mr. Nordstrom," she said, her lips without their usual smile. "I have some coffee on the back of the stove. Would you like a cup?"

Soon Mama was back with a plate of cookies, cups, and saucers. The strands of hair that had fallen around her face during supper were now in place.

When Mama and Mr. Nordstrom pulled up chairs at the table, he took a long swallow of coffee, then coughed.

Burned his tongue! thought Kate. She almost felt glad for his discomfort. As he quickly set down his cup, it rattled in the saucer.

Mama offered no sympathy. "You shouldn't have come, Mr. Nordstrom."

"I wanted to, Mrs. O'Connell," he answered, his voice just as stiff as Mama's. As he poured the coffee into his saucer, Kate saw determination in his eyes.

"My daughter was forward," said Mama, her voice soft and embarrassed. "I didn't know what she had done."

Mr. Nordstrom's low, steady voice was harder to hear. Just barely Kate picked out a word now and then. Back and forth he and Mama talked.

Then Mr. Nordstrom's words were clear. "I need a wife. Maybe you need a husband. My children need a mother. Maybe Kate needs a father."

For the first time Mama laughed. "She needs a father all right. One that takes her over his knee!"

Mr. Nordstrom's deep laugh joined Mama's. "And how about you?" he asked gently.

"I was happy before—" Mama stopped, and Kate leaned closer to the door, straining to hear.

"Before your husband died?"

Slowly Mama nodded, but didn't meet Mr. Nordstrom's eyes. Kate wished she knew what Mama really wanted to say.

Mr. Nordstrom seemed to guess. "And you'd like to marry a man you love."

Mama looked up, surprise in her blue eyes. "Yah," she said softly, sounding Swedish again.

Standing suddenly, Mr. Nordstrom strolled over to the window. For a long time he gazed down into the street. Kate knew there was only one thing to see—the gas streetlight. Yet Mr. Nordstrom looked down as though his life depended on it.

Then he seemed to make up his mind. Turning, he walked over to stand in front of Mama. There he waited until she looked into his eyes.

"How we met isn't what's most important," he said. "We can help each other."

He cleared his throat. The words seemed hard for him. "I can't promise that you'll love me. But we were friends before you found out what Kate did. Shall we start over again?"

For a long minute there was no sound in the room. Kate waited, afraid to breathe. Mama looked at Mr. Nordstrom as though thinking about what he'd said. Then she nodded and smiled.

"It's warm for February," said Mr. Nordstrom. "Let's take a walk."

Mama nodded again and stood up. Quickly she moved across the sitting room to the bedroom. Kate scrambled to her feet, but not fast enough. As Mama swung wide the door, it slammed into Kate. Mama didn't seem surprised to find her there.

As Mama and Mr. Nordstrom left for their walk, a scared feeling started in the pit of Kate's stomach. No one needed to tell her. Mama and Mr. Nordstrom would get married. What would it really be like living in a wilderness?

4

The Blueberry Special

*W*ill Mr. Nordstrom's children like me?" Kate asked Mama as they waited on the platform of the train depot.

That morning, Kate, Mama, and Mr. Nordstrom had boarded a Northern Pacific train and traveled north to Rush City. Now Mama's new husband was buying tickets for another train, the Blueberry Special, which would take them into northwest Wisconsin.

Kate shivered in the March wind, but the coldness was in her heart. "What will his children be like?" she asked Mama for the one hundredth time.

For the one hundredth time Mama answered, "As soon as we get to Grantsburg you'll find out!"

Train tickets were expensive, so Mr. Nordstrom's children had stayed on the farm when he came to marry Mama. One moment Kate felt impatient to meet them. The next moment she dreaded the idea. Her scared feelings wouldn't go away.

Lost in thought, she didn't notice a man hurrying around the corner of the depot. Bumping into Kate, he almost knocked her down.

"Pardon me, miss," he said as she caught herself. But the

apology didn't reach his gray eyes.

Without waiting to see if she was all right, the man hurried off, his shoes clicking on the wooden platform. Kate watched him go. Then a cart piled high with luggage rumbled between them.

On one end of the cart sat Mama's wooden trunk from Sweden. Two men grabbed the leather handles and swung it through the wide door of the baggage car.

The trunk was heavy, Kate knew. When Mama sold everything she could to pay the rent, only a little money was left over. The rest of their possessions she packed in the trunk.

The cold March wind stung Kate's eyes, but it wasn't the wind that brought tears. Somehow the trunk seemed like home, a home that was packed away. Yet Mama couldn't pack away Kate's feelings.

By now Kate knew even more about Wisconsin, and her thoughts spilled out. "Sarah said there're just log cabins in Wisconsin."

Mama laughed. "Mr. Nordstrom lives in a white frame house."

Kate didn't believe her. "In winter the wind blows through the cracks between the logs. In summer bugs crawl in."

Mama laughed again. "Oh, Kate."

"Sarah says there won't be any other people around for miles. Just bears. Lots of bears." Kate felt sure Sarah was right about that too.

But Mama seemed undisturbed. Her cheeks were still flushed, her blue eyes happy. Yesterday she and Mr. Nordstrom had stood before Pastor Munson as he married them.

Mama had asked Kate to stand up with them—to be her maid of honor. Mama's smile was soft as she looked into Mr. Nordstrom's eyes and said, "I do!" Kate knew Mama meant that promise to last forever. Mr. Nordstrom's "I do!" was even stronger.

Kate had tried to put on a smile, but needed to swallow her anger. "I'll never learn to play the organ in a wilderness!" she nearly cried out. Then she thought of her friends. *I might never see Sarah and Michael again*.

When Kate told them goodbye, she felt as if she were going

off to the end of the world. *Maybe I am.* Remembering her new brothers and sister, she wondered, *Will they like me?* Kate felt hollow inside, scared about starting a new life.

"Mama? Will you tell me about Daddy?" Kate's voice sounded small and uncertain.

"Again?" asked Mama.

"Again," answered Kate.

As though guessing how Kate felt about Mr. Nordstrom, Mama sighed. Yet she told the story once more. Kate listened the way she had since she was a little girl.

"Brendan and I met on the day I was going to buy a ticket and go back to Sweden," Mama began. "He lived at the boardinghouse where I worked as a maid."

Mama's eyes grew warm with remembering. "He came from Ireland about the time I came from Sweden. Swedes said to me, 'You're not going to marry an Irishman?' And the Irish told him, 'You're not going to marry a Swede? A good-lookin' lad like you?' Brendan always smiled and told them, 'She's one grand block of a woman.' "

Mama laughed and sounded young again. "So marry we did, and I never was sorry. When you were born, people asked, 'Is she going to speak Irish or Swedish?' Your daddy told them, 'This little colleen? This little girl is American!' And American you are!"

For a moment the silence was long between them. Then without thinking, Kate spoke her mind. "He's so different. Mr. Nordstrom's so different from Daddy."

"Yah," answered Mama, and her chin shot up. "But remember, young lady, different doesn't mean wrong!"

Instantly Kate felt ashamed. *I suppose I should feel grateful.* She remembered their long, hard winter. *I should feel grateful that Mr. Nordstrom wants to take care of us.* Instead, Kate's anger about moving boiled up like the clouds of smoke billowing from the steam engine.

The conductor interrupted her thoughts. "All ah-boooarrrd! All ah-boooarrrd!"

Mr. Nordstrom returned then and helped Mama and Kate up the steps of the passenger car. Near the back was a wood stove, and he led them toward its warmth. Kate dropped into the seat opposite Mr. Nordstrom and Mama.

Sliding over to the window, Kate pulled up the green shade and looked out. Near the track stood the large water tank from which men filled the engine. As Kate watched, the men swung the spout out of the way.

Inside the train, signs lined the wall near the ceiling. A big one proclaimed: WARNING: SPITTING AND SMOKING PROHIBITED. FINES AND IMPRISONMENT FOR VIOLATION. COOPERATION OF ALL PASSENGERS IS REQUESTED IN ORDER TO REDUCE THE SPREAD OF VICIOUS GERMS.

Kate looked around and couldn't see anyone spitting or smoking. But she did see the well-dressed man who had bumped into her. He was hurrying onto the train, his shoes clicking as he came to the back of the car.

Removing his spotless hat, he put it in the overhead rack, then sat down across the aisle. Settling himself, he unfolded a newspaper and started to read.

After a final "All ah-boooarrrrd!" the train groaned and slid into motion. Couplers clanked against each other; then Kate felt the cars even out. Moments later, the engine chugged onto the trestle across the St. Croix River. Looking down, Kate caught her breath. Directly below, as though there was nothing between her and the water, the river's strong current flowed black and free. Great chunks of ice, heaped up by the wind, rested against the Wisconsin side.

Mr. Nordstrom leaned around Mama to see. "Lumberjacks will send logs down soon. From shore to shore the river will be full."

Mama was full of questions, wanting to know everything about the new land in which they'd live. But Kate pretended she didn't care.

"Why did you have to drag us off to Wisconsin?" she wanted to say each time she glanced at Mr. Nordstrom.

But Mama had grown up on a farm and looked forward to living on one again. Today it seemed all the strain of the past year was gone from her face. Her hair looked golden and her eyes sparkled as she asked Mr. Nordstrom, "Why do they call this train the Blueberry Special?"

"Blueberries grow wild along here," he explained, his brown head close to Mama's blond one. "People come from all over to pick them. In just one week of blueberry season, a thousand bushels of berries can be shipped from Grantsburg."

Kate flipped her braid over her shoulder. Unwilling to talk with Mr. Nordstrom, she turned her head and looked out the window. Out of the corner of her eye she saw Mr. Nordstrom look at Mama as though asking a question.

Turning back, Kate saw Mama roll her eyes and shrug her shoulders. Kate pretended she didn't notice. Looking out the window once more, she felt pleased with herself. *I'm making it hard for them.* There was nothing Mama disliked more than when Kate acted sullen.

But Mr. Nordstrom looked calm and untroubled. "Another fifteen minutes and we'll be in Grantsburg," he said, breaking a silence.

As the train clacked along, billows of smoke rolled past and sifted through the closed windows. Soon Kate felt tired and dirty. Still she gazed out the window, her back straight and re-sentful.

After a time she looked back and saw the man across the aisle lean toward Mr. Nordstrom. "Do you live in Grantsburg?" he asked.

Mr. Nordstrom shook his head. "South of it. Down by Trade Lake," he answered, introducing himself.

"Fred Eberly," the man replied, extending his hand. Parted in the middle, his light brown hair was slicked close to his head. His darker brown handlebar moustache waved out against cheeks that seemed too white.

"New in the area?" asked Mr. Nordstrom.

"I'm a salesman," the other man explained. "Three or four times a year I bring goods in my trunk and take a room at the Antler's Hotel. Merchants look at my samples and order what they want."

While Mr. Nordstrom talked with him, Kate watched Mr. Eberly. In spite of his nice suit and slicked-back hair, the man's gray eyes looked stormy. Suddenly Kate remembered Daddy's warning to stay away from strangers. Without understanding why, she felt uncomfortable.

As the train slowed to a crawl, the conductor walked through the car. "Grantsburg! End of the line!"

The tracks edged along the side of a grist mill and the river. When the engine pulled into the station, excitement clutched Kate's stomach. Standing up, she headed down the aisle, then remembered a bag she'd left under the seat. Turning quickly, she almost crashed into Mr. Eberly.

"Watch it! Watch it!" he warned, his gray eyes cold in the face that seemed too white.

Kate drew back, surprised at the salesman's rudeness after the way he talked with Mr. Nordstrom. Slipping around him, Kate found her bag, then turned and started once more toward the door. Ahead of her, Mr. Eberly dropped his spotless hat on his slicked-back hair. His shoes clicked as he left the train.

Outside, Kate found Mr. Nordstrom looking around eagerly. "I asked them to be here when the train came in," he told Mama and Kate.

Kate knew Mr. Nordstrom meant his children. Whenever he wrote, he told Mama about Anders and Lars and Tina. Anders took care of the farm when Mr. Nordstrom came to Minneapolis.

"I'll look for them," he said now. "Maybe Anders misunderstood where we're supposed to meet."

As he hurried away, Kate and Mama followed him off the platform to the wooden boardwalk leading toward a row of buildings. Looking up and down the street, Kate saw no one that could be Mr. Nordstrom's children.

Turning back toward the train, she watched two men unload the baggage. Then Kate gasped. "Oh, my goodness!" Coming their way was the tallest man she had ever seen.

Gazing at his feet, Kate wondered, *How does he manage to buy big enough shoes?*

Then she noticed his long blue coat with gold buttons down the front and a silver star on his chest. "Is he the village marshal?" she whispered to Mama.

"Don't stare, Kate," Mama whispered back.

But Kate couldn't help herself. She had never seen such long arms and big hands.

Though short for her age, Kate knew her own height made little difference. In comparison with the village marshal, even the trainmen seemed small.

As the man moved closer, Kate tipped back her head to see. His eyes and mouth and nose were enormous. Then the big man smiled and stretched down his hand to say hello.

As Kate put her hand within his, it seemed lost. Yet strangely enough, she did not feel afraid. Instead, she looked up into kind blue eyes.

Kate didn't understand his Swedish, but Mama did. "This is Mr. Gustaf Anderson," she told Kate.

"Big Gust," he corrected, his large mouth breaking into a smile. Turning to Mama he spoke again in Swedish. *"Välkommen!"*

It sounded like *Vel comb in,* and Kate knew he was welcoming Mama, telling her Carl Nordstrom was a lucky man.

While Mama and Big Gust talked, the trainmen finished unloading the baggage car. A drayman pulled his horse and wagon near the platform and loaded a large wooden trunk.

"That's ours!" Kate exclaimed. But Mama and Big Gust were talking.

As Kate watched, Mr. Eberly climbed up and dropped onto the wagon seat. The drayman followed and clucked the horse. Pulling away from the train, he headed down the street next to the boardwalk where Kate stood.

Instantly Kate swung into motion. Forgetting everything else, she started toward the wagon. "That's our trunk!" she called out. "You've got Mama's trunk!" But the driver didn't stop.

Running as fast as she could, Kate left the walk and tore into the street. Just then the horse picked up speed. Too late Kate looked up. Instantly she saw her mistake. In another second the big horse would pound down upon her.

Fear shot through Kate as the drayman yanked back on the reins. Rearing up, the horse whinnied and pawed the air.

Kate froze, unable to move.

5

Big Brother

*F*or a moment the large hooves hung above Kate. She opened her mouth to scream, but no sound came. The next instant she felt strong arms lift her high and swing her out of the way.

The horse whinnied again, then dropped to the ground where moments before Kate had stood. As its hooves struck the earth, Kate shuddered.

Big Gust's large eyes looked concerned. "Little girl?"

"I'm *not* a little girl!" Kate told him. "I'm a big one!" But right now she didn't feel twelve years old. The stiffening in her legs was gone, and she felt weak.

Then she remembered why she tried to stop the horse. "They've got Mama's trunk."

Big Gust turned to the wagon, and Kate pointed. "See the red rose painted on the side?"

The village marshal nodded. "Yah."

"And look at the top."

With the trunk in the wagon, Kate couldn't see the words. But she felt sure that Big Gust could.

She was right. From his seven-foot, six-inch viewpoint, Big Gust read the name. "Ingrid Lindblom."

"That's Mama," explained Kate. "Before she married Daddy."

Big Gust turned to the men in the wagon. "Better take it back," he said.

The drayman's face was red. "I'm sorry. My mistake."

As the drayman turned the wagon, Kate saw Mr. Eberly looking at her. His stormy gray eyes made her uncomfortable again. *He's angry*, she thought. *Why's he mad at me?*

Then Mr. Eberly smiled and lifted his hat toward Big Gust. Kate decided she had imagined things. Yet her uneasiness wouldn't go away.

Turning his wagon, the drayman headed back to the train depot. Kate reached the platform almost as soon as he did. Sure enough, there was another wooden trunk. Except for the rose, it looked just like Mama's.

Mr. Eberly and the drayman climbed down and switched trunks. As they drove off again, Mama turned to Big Gust. "I can't thank you enough," she said, her words a jumble of Swedish and English.

As he left them, Mama pulled Kate over to a bench. Tears spilled onto her cheeks. "Oh, Kate, you're safe!"

The warmth of being loved welled up inside Kate. All the anger she'd felt that morning disappeared. Seeing Mama upset brought a tightness to Kate's throat. She couldn't speak. Not yet.

"Why did you run out in front of the horse?" Mama's voice shook with fright at the thought of the near disaster Kate had had.

Kate swallowed. "The picture," she said finally. "I didn't want them to take your picture."

For a moment Mama looked blank. "The picture?" Then her blue eyes cleared. "The picture of my family?"

Kate nodded. "With your sister holding *your* picture."

Mama sighed. "Kate, you're more important than *any* picture. Besides, it's not in the trunk."

Picking up the carpetbag at her feet, Mama opened it. Inside, carefully wrapped in towels, was the picture Kate tried to save. "I didn't want to take a chance in case the trunk was lost," Mama explained.

Then she sighed. "I think God should have warned me when

you were born." Mama's lips quivered as she tried to smile. "A big thing in a small package you are. Always leaping before you look."

Kate grinned and tossed her long black braid over her shoulder. "I'll try to be more careful," she promised solemnly. "I'll really try."

Only a few people remained on the platform, waiting for rides. As Kate and Mama sat down on the bench, trainmen disconnected the engine from the cars. Soon the engine sat alone on a piece of track above a shallow pit.

Then, using long levers, two men pushed the segment of track in front of the engine. Slowly the track moved, and with it, the engine! Walking in a half circle, the men pushed the track around until the engine faced the direction from which it came.

Mama laughed, and her voice sounded almost normal. "That Blueberry Special is really special!"

It felt good to hear Mama laugh. "Maybe it's going to be all right," said Kate and saw Mama's surprised look. "Maybe living in Wisconsin won't be so bad after all."

Then Mr. Nordstrom was back. "I found them! With the warm weather the roads thawed out. There's been rain for three days."

As Mr. Nordstrom waited, two children caught up. "Anders is with the horses," he explained. "But here are Tina and Lars." With a hand on the shoulder of each child, Mr. Nordstrom drew them forward, looking proud.

Lars bowed to Mama, then stared at Kate. Beneath a warm jacket, he was dressed in his Sunday best. But his knickerbockers had mud on them and his boots were wet, as though he'd just stopped at a pump.

A tuft of hair stood up at the back of his red head. Among his freckles, his blue eyes sparkled with mischief.

Just looking at Lars, Kate thought, *He'll put frogs in my bed.*

Tina's hair was white-blond, and the part crooked. Pulled back tightly, her lopsided pigtails looked as though whoever braided them wasn't used to little girl's hair. Now she tugged on one of those braids, putting the end in her mouth.

Tina curtsied to Mama. Turning to Kate, Tina smiled, and

sunlight seemed to dance from within.

Kate liked the little girl immediately. As though sensing it, Tina reached out a hand and tucked it inside Kate's. "My big sister?" she asked.

"Your big sister," answered Kate. She squeezed Tina's hand and felt a squeeze back.

"There's Anders now," said Mr. Nordstrom.

Coming down the street was a team of work horses and a farm wagon driven by a blond muscular boy. Seeing him, Kate smoothed her dress and wished she didn't look so rumpled. Quickly she pushed back the wisps of hair that escaped her braid.

Pulling the reins, Anders stopped the horses, then jumped down and tied them to a post. Like the other children, he wore his Sunday best. His boots also were wet. But unlike Lars, Anders had long trousers. Kate wondered if he was too tall for the knickerbockers usually worn by boys his age.

As Anders bowed to Mama, his thatch of blond hair fell over his forehead. His wide shoulders stretched the seams of his heavy coat.

When he turned to Kate, she said hello in her most grown-up voice. But then, seeing a streak of mud across his face, she smirked, trying not to laugh.

Anders' gaze met hers. With a quick swipe he wiped his hand across his face. The streak widened. Kate snickered.

Anders drew himself up to his full height. His eyes flashed, and his lips tightened as though holding back what he wanted to say. Without speaking, he turned away.

Each grasping an end, Anders and his father lifted the heavy trunk as though it were empty and set it in the wagon. Tina and Lars scrambled in toward the front, and Kate followed, sitting down on the straw. Mr. Nordstrom helped Mama climb up to the wagon seat, and Anders untied the horses. Without looking at Kate, he took the seat next to Mama.

Mr. Nordstrom flicked the reins, and the big horses headed down the dirt street.

Kate turned to Lars. "How far is it?"

"To the farm? Almost eleven miles, and it's bad."

"Bad? What do you mean?" Kate's stomach had settled down. Now it churned again. "Are there bears?"

"Nahhhh," Lars answered, his voice filled with disgust. "Mud. Mud the whole way."

Soon Kate discovered what he meant. As they left Grantsburg, deep ruts filled the roads. Often the ruts widened into large potholes. Even with straw on the bottom of the wagon, Kate soon felt sore from bouncing around.

Whenever he could, Mr. Nordstrom left the road and drove into a field to avoid the ruts. Yet in most places the forest grew up to the dirt track. Overhanging limbs snatched at the wagon.

As the miles fell away, Kate stared at the back of Anders' blond head. Mama and Mr. Nordstrom asked him questions, and the three laughed together. Kate felt left out.

"How old are you, Tina?" she asked, trying to get the four-year-old to talk.

Tina's eyes widened as she nibbled the end of her braid. When the little girl shrugged her shoulders, Kate turned to Lars.

"Speak Swede," he said.

"Swede? But she spoke English."

"Papa learned her those words," answered Lars, the tuft of red hair sticking up at the back of his head. "That's the only English she knows."

"And you?"

"Learned it at school. If we speak Swede, teacher makes us stay after."

Suddenly Kate could no longer ignore all the scared feelings she'd pushed aside. *I have a sister, and I can't even talk to her?* Once more she turned toward Mama and Mr. Nordstrom and Anders. Their laughter made Kate feel even worse.

"And you, Lars? How old are you?" she asked, unwilling to be left out of everything.

"Eight," answered Lars. When he added nothing else, Kate fell silent, too discouraged to think of more to say.

Glancing up, she saw Anders turn back and look at her. As their gaze met, he looked away. "Dumb boy!" Kate told herself. She felt sorry she'd snickered about the mud on his face, yet angry that Anders paid no attention to her.

For some time they traveled, the sharp wind whipping around them. Then grayness replaced the afternoon sun. As the miles fell behind them, the clouds thickened, and the wind grew even colder. Kate and Tina pulled a heavy horse blanket over their shoulders. Mama joined the girls under the blanket, and Lars crawled onto the seat next to his brother.

With dusk came a cold drizzle. Mile by mile, the roads grew worse. As the dampness seeped through the heavy blanket into her clothing, Kate felt the cold enter her bones.

Once Mama asked, "How much farther?"

Mr. Nordstrom answered, "Four more miles."

Mama pulled Tina onto her lap. Both of them looked as miserable as Kate felt.

Kate shivered, and the coldness would not leave. When her teeth started to chatter, Anders turned around. "Your teeth rattling in your head, Kate?"

Behind Mr. Nordstrom's back, Kate made a face. Anders grinned, but Mr. Nordstrom's look silenced him.

The big work horses leaned forward as mud sucked at their feet and splattered their coats. Often their ears turned toward Mr. Nordstrom's voice. "Com'on, Dolly. Com'on, Florie," he encouraged.

Just then the back right wheel dropped into a deep hole. As the wagon lurched, Mama's trunk slid, crashing against the end of the wagon.

"Get over! Get behind me!" Mr. Nordstrom's voice was urgent.

Quickly Mama and Kate and Tina crawled to the left, putting their weight in the front corner. The horses strained, but the wagon did not budge. As they tilted at a sharp angle, Tina began to cry.

We're going to tip! Kate bit her lip to keep from crying out as Tina had.

Mama hugged Tina close, trying to shush her. Suddenly Kate remembered Mama's carpetbag and reached out, rescuing it before it went over the side.

As Mr. Nordstrom and Anders climbed down, the wagon tipped farther. Reaching the ground, they sank into the mud.

The road seemed bottomless. Anders started toward the back of the wagon. Step by slow step he moved, searching for footing. Once he slipped and nearly went down. As he grabbed on to a wheel, the mud oozed over the top of his boots.

At the back of the wagon, Anders picked up heavy planks. Carrying them forward, he placed them in front of the wheels. Then, the mud sucking his boots with each step, he worked his way to the front of the horses.

Watching him, Kate guessed how Anders had gotten mud on his face. *I wish I could tell him I'm sorry.* Kate felt embarrassed that she'd laughed. But Anders avoided her eyes.

At the end of the wagon, Mr. Nordstrom pushed a pole under the back right wheel. "Ready?" he called out.

Anders grabbed hold of Dolly's bridle. "Ready! Giddyup," he urged the horses. "Com'on, Dolly. Com'on, Florie. Dig in. Giddyup!"

The mares strained forward, heat from their bodies steaming upward. The wagon tilted even more. Frantically Kate clung to the side until her fingers grew numb. There was nothing she wanted less than to be dumped out in the mud.

"Just a minute!" called Mr. Nordstrom. "Lars, you take the horses."

Lars crawled down into mud over his knees and struggled forward. Anders slogged past him to the back of the wagon, still without looking at Kate. There he bent down, his shoulder against the end gate. "Ready!"

Unable to reach Dolly's bridle, Lars took the reins. "Giddyup!" he called out, sounding like his big brother. "Com'on, Dolly! Com'on, Florie!"

Mr. Nordstrom leaned down on the pole, giving it his entire weight. Anders pushed against the wagon. Harnesses creaked as the horses strained forward. This time the wagon lurched out of the hole.

When the horses reached firmer ground, Lars stopped them. Anders dropped the mud-covered planks into the back of the wagon. Breaking off a branch at the side of the road, he tried to wipe the mud off his clothes. Even his blond hair had mud in it.

In the dusk Kate watched him scowl. Once he looked her

way, then glanced away. As Anders climbed onto the wagon seat, Kate did not laugh.

Soon the grayness of day merged with the blackness of night. To Kate, used to the gas streetlights of Minneapolis, the darkness seemed to settle in around them. Mr. Nordstrom gave the horses their head, and they kept moving.

It seemed that hours passed before the rain stopped. As the clouds scattered and the moon broke free, they left the road for a wagon track. The stars came out and the wind quickened, whispering in the trees around them.

When Dolly and Florie started up a long hill, they picked up speed. Mr. Nordstrom turned toward Mama. "We're almost home."

Then, out of the darkness rose the shape of buildings on both sides of the track. Mr. Nordstrom stopped the horses and lit a lantern. It *was* a white frame house after all. Yet by now Kate felt too cold and tired to care.

Inside, the fire in the wood stove had gone out. The house seemed as damp as the outside. To Kate, it was one more misery on top of the long awful day.

I don't want to live here! Kate wished she could shout it out. *I want the gas streetlights of Minneapolis. I want our warm little rooms. I want busy, cobblestone streets. I want my friends.*

Even Mama seemed quiet, no longer the glowing bride of yesterday. Kate didn't want to look at her. *If only we could go back to Minneapolis. I wonder what terrible things will happen tomorrow?*

6

Trapped!

*C*ock-a-doodle-doooo!

Kate rolled over, not sure where she was. Through the haze of half-sleep, she remembered yesterday. *Maybe coming to Windy Hill Farm was a nightmare. Maybe it was a nightmare that Mama married Mr. Nordstrom.*

But the rooster crowed again. Cock-a-doodle-doooo! Kate couldn't ignore him. The farm was real all right.

In the bed next to her, Tina stirred, opened her eyes, and smiled. In that moment Kate's feelings changed. *Maybe it won't be so bad after all.* She felt warm with the friendliness of the little girl.

My sister, Kate told herself as Tina closed her eyes and rolled over. Each time Kate repeated those words the relationship seemed more real and more special. Yet she couldn't understand Tina's Swedish.

Quietly Kate slipped out of bed. The room she and Tina shared was on the end of the house and had windows facing two directions. On one side the windows overlooked the porch and the wagon track that circled the front and side of the house. Beyond that track lay the furrows of a plowed field. Farther away, tall trees stood at the edge of a steep hill. Three bee hives stood near the trees.

45

Outside a window on the other side of the room grew a large pine. The long branches with their soft, green needles reached out to the house, almost touching it. From the other window on that side Kate saw the wagon track fork off to the right and the edge of the hill.

From this height, Kate looked across the wide expanse of what she knew must be Rice Lake. On this March morning the lake was still frozen. On its far side, hills and valleys stretched off to the horizon.

Then, as Kate stood at the window, she felt a small hand within hers. Tina tugged, and Kate guessed the little girl wanted to show her around.

They dressed quickly, and the four-year-old led Kate into the hallway. The night before, Kate had been too tired to notice the other rooms on this floor—a storeroom and the bedroom Lars and Anders shared. Already, both boys were gone.

At the bottom of the stairs Kate saw a door leading outside. But Tina turned to the right and took Kate through the front room into the dining room. There one door opened into a bedroom, another door into the kitchen.

They found Mama searching the pantry. Seeing Tina and Kate, Mama looked relieved. After saying good morning to both girls, she spoke to Tina in Swedish. Kate guessed Mama needed help in finding things. Just the same, Kate felt left out again.

Slipping through the kitchen door, she wandered outside. Nearby stood a pump, and beyond that a summer kitchen. From Mama, Kate knew that when the weather grew hot, farm families cooked and ate in these little buildings. That kept the bigger house cool for sleeping.

The rain of the night before was gone and the air sweet with the smell of spring. Kate crossed the dirt road to a building set on the edge of the hill. Going inside, she found it had large bins for storing the summer's harvest.

Beyond the granary, chickens ran around a hen house, scratching the ground. As Kate walked among them, they scattered. Then she came to the log barn.

The closest door stood open to the morning sunlight. Inside, log beams stretched across the ceiling. As her eyes adjusted to the dimmer light, Kate saw a dog bringing cows through another door.

"Woof!" it barked, nipping heels to move the cows along. As Kate watched, each cow entered a stall as though knowing where she belonged. The dog turned to face Kate. "Woof!" it barked again, more sharply.

Kate stiffened. The dog moved closer, and Kate's muscles tightened.

Just then Anders dropped down a ladder at the far end of the barn. Dressed in overalls, he held a pitchfork in one hand. Putting it down, he came forward.

"Lutfisk!" Anders called. The dog ran to him. "Good dog. Sit."

Immediately Lutfisk sat, and Anders knelt down to scratch behind the dog's ears. The dog's hair was brown with black and white markings. As he petted the dog, Anders' eyes filled with pride. "You don't have to be afraid of him."

"I'm not!" said Kate, though she felt relieved that Anders was there.

"Oh?" he drawled. A slow grin lit his face. "Could have fooled me."

"I'm *not* afraid!" Kate said again. Coming forward slowly, she reached out, gingerly patting the dog's back. "What did you call him?"

"Lutfisk," answered Anders. "You know, *lute fisk*." He said the word slowly.

"Oh," answered Kate. "I know what you mean." She hated the smell of the dried cod that Swedes soaked in lye and ate at Christmas.

"Good stuff, huh?" Anders asked, his voice enthusiastic.

Kate held her nose. "Yah. Good stuff."

Anders still petted the dog. "Got him for Christmas a couple years back. He got into the lutefisk and gobbled it up before I found him."

Turning to the dog, Anders lifted his right arm, and pointed at the door. "Go get Bess." Lutfisk headed outside.

"One cow missing," explained Anders.

"And Lutfisk will find her?"

"Yup. He brings 'em all in. I trained him myself."

Anders spoke good English, and Kate knew he'd learned it at school. She felt relieved that he seemed to have forgotten yesterday. Instead, he looked eager to show her around.

"Want to see Rosie?"

"Rosie?" asked Kate.

"My pig," Anders told her.

"Yours?"

"Papa's fattening another one for the family." Anders led Kate to a pen at the end of the barn. "Got her as a runt 'cause Papa knew she'd die otherwise. See how she's growing? I'm fattening her up for the Burnett County Fair."

"The fair? How come?"

Anders' look told Kate he certainly thought she was a dumb girl. Just the same he explained. "To get a blue ribbon. If I get first, I'll get a better price. If I get enough money selling her, I'll buy a heifer."

"A heifer?"

Anders rolled his eyes, and Kate knew she'd asked another dumb question. "A female calf. Then I'll fatten her up. If I'm lucky and have some extra money, I'll trade the heifer for a filly."

"A filly?"

"Yup. My very own horse."

Anders went back to the cows, pulled up a three-legged stool, and started milking. As milk streamed into the pail, Kate's gaze shifted to Lutfisk. He'd brought in the last cow and seemed satisfied that his work was done. Dropping on the dirt floor behind Anders, he rested his head on his paws. His brown eyes turned toward Kate.

She didn't see Anders' grin until too late. Moving his hands slightly, he directed a stream of milk to hit her face.

Kate sputtered. "Hey! What're you doin'?"

Anders laughed. This time the milk reached her eye. Kate squeezed her eyes shut and wiped them with her fists.

Anders hooted. "Open your mouth!"

Opening her eyes instead, Kate saw his shoulders shake with laughter. "Open your mouth yourself!" she spit out. "And put your foot in it!"

Dodging, she missed the next stream of milk and headed for the door. "Stupid boy!" she flung back. *I'll show him!* Heading into the bright sunlight, Kate felt determined. *If he doesn't want me around, I sure don't want to be there!*

Kate's anger stayed with her as she continued exploring. Beyond the barn was a pasture, the grass still soft and wet from melting snow and three days of rain. Large tree stumps, some four and five feet across, dotted the field.

On the far side of the pasture, the woods began again, and Kate started toward them. As she moved closer, she saw a tree with branches low enough for climbing.

Maybe it'd be a good hiding place when I don't want to talk to that stupid Anders. Kate's scared, lost feeling was back again.

Heading for the tree, she walked quickly. Partway across the field, Kate stopped. What was that? Close to the tree, on the edge of the woods, the bushes moved. Still leafless from winter, the bare branches shook as though something touched them.

Is it the wind? It can't be. There's not even a slight breeze.

Then Kate noticed something else. In a hollow of the tree, where a large branch met the trunk, something glittered in the sun. Again she started out, her curiosity mounting.

But the next moment she stopped in her tracks. Something stood behind the leafless bushes—something black. Something as tall as a man standing up.

"A bear!" In her panic Kate spoke aloud. Her stomach tightened. "Sarah said there'd be bears!"

As she tried to decide what to do, Kate heard a snort behind her. She whirled. "Oh, no!"

A short distance away, a large animal pawed the wet ground. Clods of grass spit out behind his hoof. As he lowered his head, the sunlight glinted on long horns.

Kate stifled a scream. Once again Sarah had warned her. Kate knew what the animal was. "A bull!"

Tossing his head, the bull tugged at the chain between the ring in his nose and a stake in the ground. His dark eyes rolled.

Kate's stomach churned. *Why didn't I see him?* More than once her temper had tumbled her into a mess, but this was the worst.

Fear filled her, blocking out the ability to think. *What can I do?*

Spinning around, Kate started to run toward the tree at the other side of the pasture. Midway she stopped, remembering the black shape in the bushes. "Trapped!" In her terror she spoke aloud. "Trapped between a bull and a bear!"

Turning back again, Kate faced the bull. His feet firmly planted on the soft ground, he swung his head from side to side. His long tongue reached out to lick his nostrils. Straining at his chain, he put himself between Kate and the barn.

Slowly, step by step, she started to circle the bull. His large eyes rolled as if he were watching every movement. His thick neck seemed as strong as an oak, his horns pointed and sharp.

Kate felt the bull's anger. As he pulled at the stake, the whites of his eyes widened.

Lifting his head once more, the bull let out a low guttural rumble. A shudder ran through Kate.

Again he tugged at the chain, tossing his huge head from side to side. Suddenly, with a mighty swing, the bull yanked the stake from the ground.

For a moment he stood there, eyeing Kate. Seeming to sense his freedom, he tossed his head once more. The chain and the stake swung wide.

Then the bull turned from Kate. His tail almost straight up in the air, he plunged away, running across the field.

Kate breathed deeply, relief flowing through every part of her body. But as she headed toward the barn, she saw the bull circling back.

Once again he faced her. Eyeing Kate, he stamped a back leg.

Kate stared, unable to move. "Help!" she wanted to scream. But no sound came. Her feet felt rooted to the ground. *I can't run!* Panic washed through her.

The bull took another step. Kate tried her feet. To her surprise, she could lift them. Slowly, step by step, she edged back.

The bull followed. With each step Kate took away, the bull moved closer. He bellowed, and the sound echoed in the hillsides.

Kate stopped, afraid to move or breathe. Once more the bull

pawed the ground. Clods of grass flew over his back. Dirt spit out, spraying a wide area behind the terrible hoof. Kate trembled. *God, what should I do?*

In the next instant her frantic thoughts became a prayer, her prayer a whisper. "Help me, God!" she pleaded. "Help!"

The moment stretched long as Kate stood there, every muscle tense. *It's hopeless. I'll never get away.*

Then she heard a voice behind her. "Stand still, Kate. Don't move."

Without turning her head, Kate knew it was Anders. With all her heart she wanted to run in his direction. Yet as she stepped back toward the sound of his voice, the bull took another step toward her.

"Did you hear me?" said Anders, his voice low but commanding. "Don't move."

Kate's knees began to shake, but she stood her ground.

"Stay there," said Anders, his voice closer. "Keep still."

Kate longed to turn around. Instead, she stared straight ahead. The bull rolled his eyes, and Kate could not stop trembling.

Then she felt, rather than saw, Anders close behind her. "When I say *run!* you must run," he said, still in a low, steady voice. "Don't look back. Just go. Get Papa. He's in the barn."

Kate wondered if her legs would carry her. In a moment she found out.

"Go!" commanded Anders.

Kate went, her feet flying across the soggy ground. Once she slipped and nearly fell. Catching herself, she ran on.

When she reached the edge of the field, she looked back. Anders had moved ahead, putting his tall body between the bull and Kate. In his outstretched hands was a pitchfork.

Kate headed for the barn. By the time she found Anders' father, she was out of breath. Unable to speak, she pointed to the field. Mr. Nordstrom started off in a run.

7

Trouble Ahead

$\mathcal{A}$s Kate watched from a distance, Mr. Nordstrom took the pitchfork from Anders. Step by step, they chased the angry animal toward the barn. Each time the bull pawed the ground, Kate's knees felt weak.

At last Anders and his father managed to shut him into a stout pen. Holding back the tears she didn't want Anders to see, Kate headed for the house.

Mama met her at the door. "Kate, what's wrong?"

When Kate told her about the bull, Mama's face turned white. "Oh, Kate! Another animal! You promised you'd be careful!"

"I know, Mama. I'm sorry."

"Sorry! That's not enough if you get killed!" Mama sounded stern. "You've got to take care of yourself." But then her voice broke. "Don't you know how important you are to me?"

Kate swallowed around the lump in her throat. "Am I, Mama?" she asked, her voice so quiet it could barely be heard. "Am I really?"

Mama's eyes widened with surprise. "Don't you know that, Kate?"

For a moment Mama stood looking at her as though searching Kate's face.

Unable to meet Mama's eyes, Kate looked down and traced an imaginary pattern with her toe.

"Oh," said Mama as if deep in thought. For a moment she was silent.

Still studying the kitchen floor, Kate tried to smile. But Mama knew her too well. "Kate, are you wondering if I have enough love to go around?"

Startled, Kate looked up. "How did you know?" she wanted to ask. Instead she glanced away.

"Look at me, Kate," said Mama in her I-mean-business voice. Gently she reached out and cupped Kate's chin in her hand. "Look at me and remember this. When I have a new husband and three new children, it doesn't mean I love you less. It means my love grows bigger to take in all of you."

"Cross your heart and hope to die?"

"Not hope to die, Kate," Mama answered gently. "I believe I'm needed around here. But I *am* telling the truth."

Mama smiled. "I'm asking the Lord for special guardian angels around you. But you've got to help them out!"

Kate laughed then, and her scared, lost feeling fell away. For the first time since Mama's wedding, Kate felt warm inside. But the fear didn't leave Mama's eyes.

Minutes later, Anders soaped and rinsed his hands in the basin just inside the kitchen door. Catching sight of Kate, he muttered under his breath, "Dumb girl!" Then he combed his blond hair, pretending he didn't see her.

But Kate heard. Worst of all, she knew he was right. She felt stupid all the way through.

She also knew she should thank Anders. He'd risked his life to save her. Yet the words wouldn't come. Instead she said, "You should have told me not to go there."

"You should have been *smart* enough to not go there," he answered.

Kate's temper flared. Suddenly she wanted to hurt him. She wanted to call him the meanest name she could think of. Something that said he was awkward and without manners, even though that wasn't true.

Then she knew what it could be—a name Sarah had taught

her. Kate lowered her voice so Mama wouldn't hear. "If you weren't such a country bumpkin, you'd have warned me."

Anders looked as if Kate slapped him. The red crept up into his face. "Next time—"

He stopped, and Kate knew Anders was very angry.

"Next time," he went on, "I'll leave you there. I'll let that ol' bull—"

Just then his father came into the kitchen, and Kate never heard what Anders would do.

After breakfast, Mr. Nordstrom took a worn Bible down from the shelf. "God *is* our refuge and strength," he read from Psalm forty-six. "A very present help in trouble. Therefore will not we fear. . . ."

The words sank deep inside Kate, touching an empty spot she always tried to push aside. At the same time she felt uncomfortable.

"The Lord of hosts *is* with us; the God of Jacob *is* our refuge—"

Wondering what Anders thought, Kate glanced his way.

Anders surprised her. He seemed to be listening.

As Kate moved restlessly in her chair, Mr. Nordstrom read on. "Be still, and know that I *am* God—"

"Be still?" Kate thought. Outwardly she stopped wiggling. Inside she squirmed.

Then Mr. Nordstrom prayed. "We thank Thee, Heavenly Father. We thank Thee for watching over Kate and Anders. We thank Thee that this is our first morning as a new family."

In that moment the tears Kate had held back welled up and spilled over. Quickly she wiped her cheeks, hoping Anders had not seen.

Mr. Nordstrom cleared his throat, then went on. "Help us, Father, to grow together as a family."

As he said, "Ah-men," Mama joined him. Quietly she stretched out her hand and covered Mr. Nordstrom's. When she smiled, the fear disappeared from her eyes.

But later that day, as Kate thought more about the bull, she wondered if God really did help her. Probably Anders just happened to come along when he did.

About suppertime it started raining again and continued all night. The following day was Sunday, and Mr. Nordstrom said the roads were too muddy to go to church. After breakfast he led them in prayer and singing. The family sang well together, but Kate wished she had an organ and could play the hymns.

When Monday morning dawned, fog hid the lake below the hill. In the silence the gray-white world seemed eerie.

Kate felt scared about starting a new school, scared about meeting the other children. *What if they don't like me? What if they all act like Anders?* She knew there was no way to get out of it, but felt more uneasy all the time. *I wish I didn't have to go.*

That morning Kate spent extra time in front of the mirror. More than once she'd been glad that Mama was a seamstress for wealthy ladies. Often they gave her leftover material. Sometimes Mama figured out a way to use two colors together and have enough for a dress.

The light blue dress Kate put on now was her favorite. As she stood before the mirror, tying her long sash, she knew she looked her best. At the same time her deep blue eyes looked scared.

Catching up the locket from Daddy, she clasped it around her neck, then went down to breakfast. There Kate discovered she and Anders and Lars would take a trail through the woods to school.

"It's shorter than walking around on the road," Mr. Nordstrom told Kate. "No one's logged there lately, so it won't have deep ruts. But where there's mud, be careful. It's as slippery as ice."

When it was time to go, Mama handed Kate her slate and a syrup pail. With a metal handle and tight-fitting lid, the pail protected her lunch from all kinds of weather.

Anders led the way outside. Without looking at Kate, he stalked off on the wagon track leading down the hill past the lake. Red-headed Lars followed, the tuft of hair standing up at the back of his head. Kate fell in behind.

His long legs stretching out, Anders set a brisk pace. With her shorter legs, Kate found it hard to keep up. Each time they came to a mudhole, she edged around it, trying to stay clean.

Sheltered by the woods, patches of snow still covered the ground. In the gray-white fog, pine trees seemed black, and tangled bushes formed hedges. All around Kate, leafless branches closed in as though unwilling to give up land for the track.

She shivered, glad for the warm coat she wore. "How far is it?" she asked the back of Anders' head.

When he didn't answer, Kate raised her voice, trying again. It was Lars who told her. "About a mile."

Before long, the track became a trail, then a path. Here and there other paths led off the main one. Soon Kate lost her sense of direction. She felt glad that Anders led them, even if his broad shoulders looked stiff and unyielding. He was still angry, Kate knew. Always his blond head faced forward as though he wanted to ignore her.

They had walked for some time when Kate heard a school bell ring. As she quickened her steps, Lars turned his freckled face toward Kate. "That's the first bell. We've got another half hour."

Soon after, they came to a high ridge where the land fell sharply away on either side of the path. Small ice-covered pools filled the hollows far below. After following the ridge for a while, Anders stopped.

Lars pointed down through trees still bare of leaves. "That's it."

At the bottom of the hill a schoolhouse stood on a rise near the windswept ice of a lake. Kate felt confused. "Is that the lake near our house?"

Lars shook his head, and his red hair fell over his eyes. "That's Spirit Lake. We live on Rice Lake. We've come through the woods between."

Without a word, Anders set off again, and Kate and Lars followed him down the hill.

At the bottom, a creek flowed between them and the schoolhouse. Swollen by rain and melting snow, the creek ran high between its banks. Kate stopped, knowing she couldn't jump across.

Then she saw the log spanning the water. Anders bounded

ahead, moving so fast he seemed to run across. Lars followed, balancing as if not giving it a thought.

Kate swallowed, but the empty feeling in her stomach didn't go away. *I can't show 'em I'm scared*, she thought. *They'll laugh at me.*

Carefully she set one foot on the end of the log. Then she looked down. The swollen creek rushed beneath her. Kate felt cold with fear.

"Come on," said Anders, speaking for the first time that morning.

Kate set down her other foot. But when she tried to pick up the first one, she couldn't move. Her foot seemed frozen to the log.

"Hurry up!" prodded Anders.

Kate felt like an ice statue. "I can't," she said finally, her words just a whisper.

Anders sounded impatient. "Come on, scaredy-cat! Won't hurt you. Just walk across."

"I can't," said Kate again. The water seemed closer now, rushing even faster. Yet somehow she felt higher above it.

"You better come or a country bumpkin will have to help you," Anders called out.

Kate felt the heat move up into her face and knew she was blushing. "I'm sorry," she said softly, still not taking her eyes away from the water.

"*Sorry!*" Anders exclaimed, but Kate was afraid to raise her eyes to his face. "Sorry, the city girl says. That's not enough." His voice changed, sounding self-important and loud. "The preacher says that when you say mean things, you're supposed to ask forgiveness."

Kate's head shot up. "Forgiveness, my foot!" Catching the grin on Anders' face, she nearly lost her balance.

"Well," drawled Anders, his voice back to normal. "I guess I'll have to help you out again."

When he jumped on the log it shook, and Kate nearly tipped off. Tucking her slate under her other arm, she gave Anders her free hand. As they started up the muddy bank on the opposite side, he let go.

Kate's feet slid from beneath her, and she fell forward on her hands and knees. Her slate and syrup pail dropped in the mud. "Oh, no!" she cried.

"Oh, no!" drawled Anders, echoing her voice.

Carefully Kate picked herself up. Her hands were brown with mud, and her long stockings looked the same. "Oh, ick!"

Taking out her handkerchief, Kate wiped her hands and knees. At least her dress and coat didn't look too bad. Gingerly she picked up the dirty lunch pail and slate.

Sliding back down the bank, Anders stretched out his hand. Once more Kate grabbed hold. As he stepped onto the dead brown grass at the top, Anders let go again.

Without warning the soft ground gave way beneath Kate, and she sat down hard. Cold mud oozed through her stockings and dress.

Helplessly she looked up, wondering if Anders had tricked her. Then she saw Lars grin and knew the answer. Anger filled her. Scrambling up, she nearly fell again.

Once on solid ground Kate stomped her feet. As she faced Anders, she exploded. "You let go on purpose!"

"Me? *I* let go on purpose? How could a country bumpkin think of a thing like that?" Anders grinned at his brother. "Lars, do you think I'd ever do something like that?"

Lars snickered, and Kate's anger grew. "You—You—" she sputtered, unable to find words terrible enough. "You're both just awful!" she stormed. "You planned this!"

Pulling up long dead grass, she tried to wipe herself off. Yet as she twisted around to look at her skirt, she felt sick. Mud covered most of her back side.

"I want to go home," she said, trying to keep her voice steady.

"You can't," answered Anders so quickly that Kate knew he meant business. "You can't walk that far when you're wet. Your clothes will ice up."

His voice softened. "Come on."

Slowly Kate followed. There was nothing she wanted less than to pass through the door of that school.

8

Spirit Lake School

 $\mathcal{A}$ s Kate entered the schoolhouse, she felt the warmth of the potbelly stove reach out to her. Rows of desks, connected one to another, stretched away to the front. Above the blackboard hung a picture of George Washington and another of Abraham Lincoln.

Seeing Kate at the door, a young-looking teacher came to meet her.

"This is Miss Sundquist," introduced Anders, his voice polite. "Katherine Nordstrom."

"Katherine *Nordstrom*?" The name jolted Kate. "I'm Katherine O'Connell!" Anders was the last person on earth she'd expect to call her *Nordstrom*.

The teacher looked at her, then at Anders. "Which is it?"

Anders shrugged and waited, watching Kate.

Kate drew a deep breath. "I'm an O'Connell," she said boldly, even though Mama had asked her to use Nordstrom.

Anders stood there watching, his blue eyes filled with laughter.

Then Kate guessed he was waiting to see if she'd tell on him. Behind her back, she clenched her fist and turned partway for Anders to see.

Anders snickered.

Miss Sundquist turned to him. "Something funny, Anders? I don't think so. Katherine looks wet and cold." Turning back to Kate, she asked, "What happened?" Concern filled her voice.

Below his thatch of blond hair, Anders' face turned solemn. Standing quietly, he stayed within earshot, as though daring Kate to put the blame on him. When she didn't, he drifted off.

Miss Sundquist led Kate to the small cloakroom. Along two outside walls were shelves for lunch pails. On the other walls hooks held coats and sweaters. "You can hang your coat here," said the teacher. "Let it dry before trying to get out the mud. But why don't you wash up at the pump? I have some towels."

Outside, Kate felt the brisk March air even more. As she dabbed mud off her long stockings, the water from the pump felt like ice. Twisting around, she tried to scrub the back of her dress. The brownish gray spot widened.

Her long sash dripped mud. Taking it off, Kate rinsed it under the pump, squeezed out the water, and retied the bow in back.

Inside once more, she felt chilled all through. For a time Kate stood with her back to the wood stove, watching the other children watch her. Gradually she grew warmer, but her stockings stayed wet and soggy. They'd take a long time to dry.

When Miss Sundquist assigned a desk, Kate sat down quickly, hoping to hide the spot on her dress.

A moment later, the teacher asked the children to stand for the pledge of allegiance. Slowly Kate slid out of her desk. Behind her, someone snickered.

"Psssst!"

Kate whirled around.

"Psssst!" The boy directly behind Kate hissed again, trying to get Anders' attention. Anders grinned at him, then tipped his head toward Kate.

Quickly Kate turned back, facing the front. It was no secret the boys were talking about her. As she sat down again, she had one thought. *What are they planning to do?*

To make matters worse, a cold wind swept through a knothole in the floor near Kate's desk. In the next hour her wet legs and feet felt icy, then numb. She shivered, biting her lips to keep her teeth from chattering. With all her heart she didn't want to stand up and get her coat.

Trying to forget her misery, Kate looked around. The strange girls made her lonesome for Sarah Livingston, so lonesome that she ached inside.

Across the aisle two girls shared a double desk. The closest one looked about Kate's age. With light brown hair and hazel eyes, she had clear skin with a dusting of freckles across her nose. When Miss Sundquist called on the girl, Kate learned her name was Josie Swenson.

Maybe I can get to know her at recess, Kate thought.

Later on, though, when she happened to look up, she caught Josie and her friend staring. They were looking at the dress Kate had proudly put on that morning.

"It's store-bought," she heard the other girl whisper. Josie nodded, then looked away.

For the first time, Kate noticed the dresses worn by the other girls. Her own looked too nice.

"Mama sewed this dress," she wanted to shout out. "I'm just like you!" But Kate knew it wasn't true. She was different.

Then she remembered something else. Quietly she took hold of the heart-shaped locket Daddy had given her and slipped the chain inside her dress. Even so, as the other girls looked her way, Kate knew it was too late. They had already noticed her jewelry.

Once again Kate felt lonesome for Sarah. "I'd like to be friends!" she wanted to tell the girls around her. Instead, she felt set apart.

"In this whole school I'm the only one with black hair," Kate muttered to herself. Her misery mounted. "I'm the only girl with one braid instead of two! I'm the only person with an Irish name!"

For a moment Kate thought about it. Then she flipped her braid over her shoulder. *And I'm going to stay that way! I'll show 'em!*

Yet before long Kate's small bit of confidence melted away. Up and down the rows one child, then another, looked her direction, then snickered. Whenever Kate heard them she wondered, *Why are they laughing at me?*

Opening a book, she pretended to read. Anders walked past and snatched the book out of her hands. His hoarse whisper reached up and down the aisle. "You're not reading, Katherine *Nordstrom.*"

With an exaggerated bow, he turned the book right side up. Erik, the boy behind Kate, laughed softly.

Then Miss Sundquist called on Kate to recite.

Kate groaned. "Do I have to?" she wanted to ask. All she could think about was the muddy spot on her dress.

Miss Sundquist called again. "Katherine, come here, please." Slowly Kate tried to stand up. She couldn't move.

Across the room a girl snickered. One child after another joined her.

Again Kate tried to stand. Yet she felt bound to her seat. She tried to twist around, but couldn't. Then she knew what was wrong. Erik had tied her sash to the desk back of her! Kate's cheeks felt warm with embarrassment as she tried to struggle free.

"Erik Lundgren, untie Kate!" ordered Miss Sundquist.

As Erik set Kate free, every child turned to watch. Slowly Kate stood up, and the children covered their mouths with their hands, hiding their laughter.

Slowly Kate walked forward, plagued by one thought: *Everyone in this whole school is watching.*

When morning recess arrived, Kate eagerly headed for the cloakroom. Yet, once outside, she faced another nightmare. In class Miss Sundquist expected the children to speak English. If they didn't, they had to stay after school. Yet when the teacher couldn't hear them, the children spoke the Swedish they weren't allowed to use during school.

At first Kate struggled, trying to understand what they said. Finally she gave up and added another misery to her list. *I'm the only one in this whole school who doesn't know Swedish!*

Dragging her feet, Kate left the play area and sat down on the porch at the front of the school. "At least Mama loves me!" she told herself, clinging to that one hope.

Around her, the other children shouted and played, but

Kate's thoughts were far away. *I wonder what Sarah's doing now—and Michael. I want to go back to Minneapolis.*

Somehow the morning passed. During lunch hour Kate couldn't get the tight-fitting lid off her syrup pail. Watching closely, she saw Josie ask the teacher for a table knife. Sliding it under the narrow edge, Josie lifted the lid in three or four places until it popped up.

Kate borrowed the knife, but still couldn't open her pail. Finally she turned to Josie. "Will you help me?"

As she showed Kate what to do, Josie smiled shyly.

"Where do you live?" Kate asked quickly, not wanting to miss an opportunity. By the time lunch hour ended, Josie seemed less afraid to be friends.

That afternoon the snickering started again. Miss Sundquist seemed as tired of it as Kate. Searching for the ringleaders, she called out, "Anders!" then "Lars!"

The two boys stood up.

"Go to the cloakroom until you stop laughing."

Lars looked scared, as though he wasn't used to this kind of punishment. Anders was a different matter. As he left his desk, he winked at Erik. Anders didn't seem to have a care in the world.

As Lars and Anders reached the cloakroom, Miss Sundquist spoke again. "Don't come back until you're through laughing!"

After that, the day went better for Kate. Finally it ended. Picking up her books, she grabbed her coat and lunch pail. Once outside, she stood for a moment on the porch, watching children scatter in all directions.

Then, rounding the corner of the school, Kate looked for Anders and Lars. No one was there.

Circling the building, Kate searched. With each step she felt more upset. Finally an awful thought dawned on her. *They're hiding from me! They're pretending they aren't here. They want to see how scared I get.*

Drawing a deep breath, she tried to look calm. *Trouble is, I am scared.*

Just thinking about finding her way through the woods filled Kate with panic. *What will I do?*

For a moment longer she stood there, then made up her mind. "Dumb boys! I'll fool 'em!" she muttered.

Certain that Anders and Lars watched from behind a bush, Kate set out. *I'm not going to let 'em laugh at me!*

Coming to the creek, she slid down the bank, but managed to stay on her feet. The icy water roared beneath the log as Kate put her foot upon it. Swallowing hard, she took one step, then a second, and a third.

To her surprise the crossing didn't seem nearly as bad as that morning. Now she had a greater fear—finding her way through the woods. As Kate reached the end of the log, she leaped onto solid ground.

"I'll show those boys," she said aloud, working up her courage. Straightening her shoulders, she tossed her head and flipped her shiny black braid.

With confident steps, she set off on the path. "I'll make it on my own," she muttered, wanting to look around to see where Anders and Lars hid. "Dumb boys!"

But at the top of the hill Kate faced a choice. The path led three different ways.

For a long minute she stood there, wondering what to do. The bright sunlight that had replaced the morning fog made everything look different.

Maybe I should go back. Half turning, Kate glanced down the hill, then noticed something.

When she looked toward the school, the trees appeared as they had that morning. Choosing the center path, Kate turned around to check herself. "I've got it!"

Starting out once more, she set a good pace and kept to it. "Dumb boys!" she said again. "I don't need 'em." Her confidence was growing.

For a time Kate followed a long ridge that dipped to lower ground. Then she came to a Y-shaped fork, one she hadn't noticed that morning. Turning around, she looked back. This time the trees didn't offer a clue.

The ground was firmer here with no footprints to follow. Kate stopped and looked around again, puzzled about what to do. Finally, she took the trail veering to the right.

The woods were more open now, and March winds had dried the ground. Kate's feet scuffled the brown leaves left by winter. But before long, the path grew faint.

Kate turned back, planning to retrace her steps. But as she looked down she could not believe her eyes. *It's gone! The path's disappeared!*

Her scared feelings returned. *How did I get here? Where am I?*

Then Kate heard the rustling of leaves. "Anders! Lars!" she called out. A squirrel scampered away.

"Anders! Lars!" she shouted again. No longer did she care if they laughed at her. "Come on out! The joke's over!"

Kate listened, then called until hoarse. No one shouted an answer. No one popped out of the bushes laughing.

Finally the terrible truth struck her. *They aren't here! They aren't hiding from me!*

Deep inside, Kate trembled. Around and around, one thought whirled in her mind: *I'm lost in these awful woods!*

9

The Mysterious Stranger

Filled with panic, Kate broke into a run. Branches reached out and whipped her face. Thorns snatched at her coat and legs.

Looking for openings between trees and bushes, Kate tumbled through. Several times she circled large clumps of growth. Finally she had to stop. She could not move ahead through the tangled brush.

Making herself stand still, she took a long, deep breath, but her panic would not go away. *Bears. Bears live in that brush.*

Behind Kate, a branch cracked, and she spun around. In that moment she remembered everything she'd ever heard about bears. "Wisconsin is a wilderness," Sarah had said. "It's filled with bears."

"Yah, we have bears," Mr. Nordstrom told Kate and Mama. "Sometimes five-hundred-pound ones."

It didn't matter that he also said, "They're more afraid of us than we need to be of them." Kate remembered only his words, "Yah, we have bears." Her stomach churning, she tried to push aside fear. But then she had another terrible thought: *What if it gets dark before I find my way?*

Like waves on a beach, panic washed over Kate, and she began to sob. "I'm scared, God!" she cried out. "Really scared." The fear in her voice echoed back.

She tried again. "This is even worse than the bull, God. Maybe you did help me then."

She found it hard to believe that the God who answered her prayers the wrong way could ever do something good. Yet she felt desperate. "If you get me out of this, God, I'll—"

Kate stopped, trying to think of a promise to trick God into helping her. Finally she had it. "If you help me, God, I'll believe you can take care of me. I'll even believe you do good things!"

For a moment Kate stood there, surrounded by silence. She wondered if she'd hear a voice telling her what to do. Now that she'd asked God for help, she felt even more scared. *Maybe God doesn't care what happens to me. Maybe He'll get even for the mean things I've thought about Him.*

Then Kate forgot the maybes. Above the sound of her heart-beat she sensed the stillness of the woods.

Something within Kate broke. She felt strange—still, the way the woods seemed now. For the first time in many months she felt quiet, even peaceful. It helped her remember the words Mr. Nordstrom read. "Be still, and know that I *am* God."

A light breeze touched Kate's face, drying her tears. She drew a deep breath, and her scared feeling slipped away. She felt sur-prised it was gone.

Then she remembered something else—something Daddy had said. "You have to face things, Kate, even though you're afraid. You have to walk straight ahead."

He'd spoken those words whenever she was afraid. Afraid of starting school. Afraid of trying something she really needed to learn. *Walk straight ahead? But how?*

Kate had heard stories about people lost in the woods. Often they walked in circles, never finding their way out. *Maybe that's what I've been doing.* Her panic started to come back, but so did her father's words. "Walk straight ahead."

How? In the stillness the word seemed to echo back.

Then Kate noticed the sun. Slowly she started out. Carefully, she picked her way around the thickets. This time she used the sun as a guide and headed in one direction.

The minutes stretched long, but at last Kate came to a path. She had no idea where it went, and whether she was going toward school or away. She just felt glad for something to follow. The path had to go somewhere.

After walking a time, Kate saw that off to the left the trees seemed thinner. Perhaps she'd be able to see something from there. Yet she felt afraid to leave the path, knowing she might not find it again.

Carefully Kate looked around. A tall oak behind her. A cluster of birch on her left. Slowly she turned, memorizing the way the trees stood. Then, counting her steps, she moved off the path.

Soon the heavy brush ended. Spying a large rock, Kate climbed onto it. Nearby, the steep hill fell away. Tall marsh grass and small trees broke through the remaining snow. Beyond was the windswept ice of a lake. It seemed familiar.

For a moment Kate thought about it, trying to jog her memory. Then suddenly it struck her. *It's Rice Lake! I know where I am!* She also felt sure she could find Windy Hill Farm. If she kept the lake on her left, she'd be home!

Taking one last look, Kate felt eager to be off. Then she heard the crack of a branch.

Kate stiffened. *Are there bears, after all?*

A second branch cracked. Then came the sound of something shuffling through the dry, dead leaves on the ground. As Kate stood there, the sound moved closer. Closer. Closer.

Kate turned, facing the direction of the sound. As she stood on the rock, she peered over a fallen oak, the dead leaves still clinging to the branches.

Along the path a man came into sight. *Whew! It wasn't a bear.*

Kate opened her mouth to call out, but something told her to be quiet. Then she saw the man's face and was glad.

Under an old hat his curly black hair hung to his shoulders. His long black beard was just as curly and looked as if it hadn't been combed for weeks. He carried a small wooden box and a shovel.

The stranger stopped and looked around. Quickly Kate knelt down behind the fallen oak.

A moment later, she heard the sound of digging. Slowly, quietly, she stood up and peered over the branches.

The man had set the box on the ground. In a small open space away from trees and bushes, he was digging a hole, his back toward Kate. His wrinkled black coat had a long tear on one sleeve.

As Kate watched, the man widened the hole and dug deeper. After a time he set his spade in the dirt and looked around. Her heart thumping, Kate ducked down. When she heard shoveling again, she stood up.

The box was gone, and the man was shoveling dirt back into the hole. Every now and then he stepped on the dirt, stomping it down to pack it. Finally he stood back, seeming to mark the hole between the clump of birch and the large oak.

Again he looked around, but this time at the ground. Breaking off brown clumps of grass left by the melting snow, he carried them to the hole. There he scattered the long strands over the dirt.

Next he collected wet, fallen leaves from under a bush and spread them over the grass. Once more he stood back, looking at his work.

Picking up his tools, the stranger set out. At a muddy spot, he stepped to one side of the path, then kept on toward Windy Hill Farm.

When Kate felt sure the stranger was gone, she retraced her steps to the path. For a moment she stood there, marking the spot between the clump of birch and the large oak. If she hadn't seen the box, she never would have guessed it was there.

Kneeling down, Kate pushed aside the leaves and dried grass. As she uncovered the place the man had dug, she found prints in the dirt. There was something different about them— different from other shoes or boots.

How can I dig up the box? One try in the firmly packed earth, and she knew it was hopeless. She'd have to come back with a shovel. *I'll get Anders. He won't be afraid.*

Quickly Kate covered the spaded earth with the dry grass

and leaves. Satisfied that she'd hidden the spot well, she headed
down the path.

At last Kate came to the logging trail, then the wagon track
that curved around the bottom of the hill near the Windy Hill
farmhouse. When she saw the spring between the road and Rice
Lake, she knew she was almost home.

Heavy beams, built around the spring like a large wood box,
caught and held the water. Kneeling down, Kate slipped her
hands into the wetness. The cold shock went all the way up her
arms. But it felt good, too, and she leaned over, lapping water
onto her face. Then, cupping her hands, she began to drink.

Finally she rocked back on her heels. For a long moment she
sat there, gazing across Rice Lake to the hills beyond.

Her fear of being lost in the woods was gone. But now Kate
felt afraid about the stranger she'd seen. *Who is he? What's in
the box he buried?* Deep in thought, she didn't hear the step
behind her. Instead, Kate felt a tap on her shoulder.

She jumped. Her heart pounded into her throat. *Had that
awful looking man come back?*

10

Bees!

*S*pringing to her feet, Kate stepped on the hem of her dress. As she whirled around, she barely heard the rip.

Anders stood there, laughter in his blue eyes. Kate's panic changed to anger. "What are *you* doing here?"

A slow grin lit his face. Reaching down, he plucked a stem of marsh grass that rose above the remaining snow. "All right that I'm here, city girl?" he asked as he began chewing the grass. "It's where I live."

Kate stomped her foot. "I know it's where you live! But what do you mean sneaking up on me like that?"

"Coming to look for you," he drawled. "Just in case you can't find your way home."

"I did just fine," Kate answered, her voice resentful. Yet she felt the blood flooding into her face. "Where were you, anyway?"

"Teacher said not to come back until we stopped laughing. Lars and I couldn't stop laughing." Anders looked as though he was heading off into laughter again. Then he winked. "So we snuck out under the shelves in the cloakroom and came home."

Kate started to smile, almost joining Anders in his laughter. Then she remembered how she felt, hemmed in on every side by bushes, lost and alone. She swallowed around the lump in her throat.

Anders' grin disappeared, and his eyes looked serious. "Forgot you might not remember your way."

"Of course I knew my way!" exclaimed Kate, hoping he wouldn't guess how scared she'd been. "Just took my time walking home."

"You're lying," Anders said calmly. "You still look scared."

Kate straightened her shoulders, trying to make herself look taller. "That's ridiculous!" she replied in her most grown-up voice. "Like I said, I had a good walk."

"Well, just checking to make sure the bears didn't get you."

Suddenly Anders leaned forward, plucked a twig off the sleeve of her coat, and handed it to her. "Got off the path, didn't you? You better wash that scratch on your cheek." Taking out a handkerchief, he dipped it in the spring and leaned forward.

Quickly Kate stepped back, out of reach. "I don't want your help!"

Anders shrugged. "All right by me. But when you wash up, why don't you get the dirt off your face?"

"The dirt?"

"Yup. The ring around the edge of your face."

Once again Kate felt the red creeping up. "Oh, you—you—" she sputtered. Turning, she stomped off toward the house.

Anders' voice followed her. "What's the matter, city girl?" Then he changed to a singsong chant. "Scare-dy-caaat, scare-dy-caaat!"

Without warning, tears welled up in Kate's eyes. She quickened her pace, keeping her back toward Anders so he wouldn't see. *Will I ever feel I belong? Will I ever feel part of this family?*

She was halfway up the steep hill when she remembered. She hadn't told Anders about the mysterious stranger. "Well, I'm not telling him now!" she muttered to herself. "He'd say, 'You're making it up 'cause you're scared!' "

His teasing rang in her ears. *"Scaredy-cat!" he calls me! Well, I had good reason to be afraid. But how can I prove it to him?*

Farther on, Kate met Lutfisk. She hadn't been near the dog

since seeing him in the barn. Today he seemed friendly, and Kate felt relieved. Kneeling, she stroked his black, brown, and white back. When he turned his head to lick her hand, she felt better. *At least one person in this family likes me!*

At the top of the hill, Mr. Nordstrom stood near the beehives, wearing a hat and veil. Aiming his smoker at the entrance of a hive, he pushed the bellows. A cloud of smoke rolled out.

Kate walked closer, and Mr. Nordstrom called to her. "Want to see?"

Thinking about how she disliked his marriage to Mama, Kate started to shake her head. Then she remembered Anders. *I'll show him I'm not a scaredy-cat!*

"Sure," she called to Mr. Nordstrom.

She still felt shy with Mama's new husband. Compared to Daddy, Mr. Nordstrom was quiet and seldom talked unless something needed saying. Yet Kate felt curious about the bees. More than that, she wanted to prove she wasn't a scaredy-cat.

"Ask your mama for some overalls and a straw hat. Tell her there's an old thin curtain in the bottom drawer in the pantry. You can use that for a veil."

Soon Kate was back. The overalls were too big, and Mama insisted that she tie string around her ankles so the bees couldn't crawl inside. On her head Kate wore a straw hat with the curtain draped around to protect her face and neck. It felt hot and clumsy, but she could see.

"Just move slow and quiet," Mr. Nordstrom told her as he took the cover off a hive.

Within the wooden box Mr. Nordstrom called a hive body were a number of frames. "Come closer," he said as she hesitated. "A sunny day like this is a good time to look."

Hundreds of bees crawled across the top of the frames, their wiggling bodies humming. Some of them flew up, heading toward Mr. Nordstrom and Kate. "Stand still," he warned. "Then they won't bother you."

As the bees buzzed around Kate's head, she flinched, wanting to run. "Can they get through my veil?" she asked, fear tightening her muscles.

Mr. Nordstrom laughed. "They seem to get through everything. But you'll be all right. Just stay quiet."

Pushing the bellows, he sent a cloud of smoke toward Kate. The bees left her, and Mr. Nordstrom turned back to the hive.

"What are you looking for?" asked Kate.

"I'm checking on the queen. This time of year she should be laying eggs."

Mr. Nordstrom pulled a frame from the center of the hive body. "See how the bees build honeycomb? All the hexagon-shaped holes? They put eggs and pollen and nectar in them." Mr. Nordstrom tipped the frame toward the sun. "Look close. There's a white line you can barely see. Like a tiny piece of thread."

Kate squinted.

"See it?"

She nodded, her interest growing.

"That's an egg," said Mr. Nordstrom, replacing the frame and picking up another. "Eggs grow into larvae." He pointed to what looked like small white worms. "Larvae grow into bees."

A strange excitement filled Kate—the excitement of knowing she could stand there in spite of her fear of being stung. *I hope Anders sees me.* Aloud she asked, "How do bees know how to do everything?"

"They have different jobs. One hive is like a whole community working together."

"All of 'em?"

Mr. Nordstrom shook his head. "Not all of them. The drones don't work. In fall, when worker bees start worrying about their food supply, they push drones out of the hive."

Kate giggled. "It's like a family. Sometimes they don't like each other."

Mr. Nordstrom looked up quickly. Replacing the cover, he moved a short distance from the hive and took off his hat and veil. "Kate, are you finding it hard to live here?"

Kate glanced away, unwilling to meet his gaze. She didn't want to answer, but Mr. Nordstrom asked again. "It's different for you, isn't it?"

Slowly Kate nodded and began pulling off the old straw hat. Suddenly all the awful feelings of the day washed over her. Falling in the mud. Being new in school. Everyone laughing. And then, getting lost in the woods because of dumb Anders. Kate was afraid to look at Mr. Nordstrom—afraid she'd cry.

"It's hard to get used to changes, isn't it?" he asked.

Surprise caught Kate off guard. Her words were out before she could stop them. "How did you know?"

Mr. Nordstrom's quiet smile reached his blue eyes. "Whether we're children or grownups, it's difficult for all of us. When we have to face new things, I mean."

He cleared his throat. "I wish for your sake your papa hadn't died—just like I wish my Anna hadn't died. But it happened to both of them. And we can't go back by just wishing."

Kate swallowed, knowing he was right, but unable to speak. Always Mr. Nordstrom seemed so quiet, as though nothing really bothered him.

"Look ahead, Kate," he said, surprising her again. "You have to go on."

"How?" she asked, the word exploding from within. It hung between them in the quiet air. Kate wished it was that simple. Inside, there was a little hollow place where her heart used to be. "How?" she asked again. She needed to know.

But Mr. Nordstrom had another question. "What means a lot to you, Kate? I know you want a real family." He grinned. "Not every day. At least, not when Anders is mean."

"How did you know?" Kate's words gave her away.

"I know Anders. He'll get over it. But at least some of the time you want a happy family. Your mama told me so. What else is important to you?"

Kate was afraid to tell him. No one had asked that question before. She hadn't told anyone, not even Mama. Yet somehow she felt she could trust Mr. Nordstrom.

"I want to play the organ," she answered finally, her voice small. But then the strength of her wish welled up, and her words tumbled out. "I want to travel around the United States, giving concerts like Jenny Lind."

"The Swedish nightingale?"

Kate nodded. "But instead of singing, I want to be an organist." Kate stopped. The words were out. She couldn't call them

back, and she felt scared. What if Mr. Nordstrom laughed?
But he didn't.

"You could learn from Mr. Peters," he said.

"Mr. Peters?"

"The organist at our church."

"You have an organ?"

"Yah, sure. The first hand-pumped organ in the county."

"You do? Here in the wilderness?"

Mr. Nordstrom's grin reached his eyes, reminding Kate of
Anders. "Well, it's not quite the end of the world."

After a moment he spoke again. "You'd have to have something to practice on. Are you willing to work to buy an organ?"

Kate gasped. "Oh yes! But it's so much money."

"Yah. But let's think. How can you earn the money?"

"I don't know," Kate answered slowly. It seemed impossible.
Yet deep inside, she felt hope for the first time. The hope that
maybe, just maybe—

"I'll think about it," she said, and Mr. Nordstrom smiled.

He picked up his smoker, and they started back to the house.
"You'll be all right, Kate. You'll earn your way with Anders."

Outside the kitchen door he spoke once more. "And when
you feel ready, I'd be honored to have you call me Papa."

11

View From the Bell Tower

*D*uring supper Kate listened to the other children call Mr. Nordstrom Papa. Since his marriage to Mama, Kate had avoided calling him by name. But that night, in the room and bed that she shared with Tina, she thought about what Mr. Nordstrom said.

Only Daddy will ever really seem like a father to me.

Yet as she lay quietly in the darkness, she thought of something. *Daddy's been dead for a year and a half now. Is it the name that matters? Or how much he loved me?*

When Mr. Nordstrom talked to me today, it was almost like hearing Daddy say, "Walk straight ahead, Kate. You have to face things, even though you're afraid."

Long ago Kate had tucked away those words in her heart. She wanted to remember Daddy saying them. She wanted to remember how it felt when he came home from work and gave her a big hug. How his eyes twinkled when he laughed, and how he sang funny songs that always made her feel better. She wanted to hold those memories of Daddy so they wouldn't slip away.

Strange, though, how more than anything he told her, she remembered him saying, "Look ahead, Kate, not back. Walk straight ahead." He had spoken those words more than once as if he knew she'd need to remember them.

But what did they mean now? Kate still felt scared about the way God answered her prayer for a husband for Mama. She still wanted to go to school with Sarah Livingston and Michael Reilly. Was that looking back?

When Tina fell asleep, Kate practiced saying *Papa* the way the other children did. She tried to fit Mr. Nordstrom's face with the name. Maybe sometime she could say Papa to him. But not yet.

Soon after, Kate drifted off to sleep. Toward morning she dreamed about bees. In her dream she stood near the hives. As she watched, honey started to flow out of the top. Spilling over the sides, the runaway honey became golden rivers along the ground.

Kate scrambled for jars. "Where are they?" she cried out. But not even Mama knew where to get enough jars.

"That's it!" Kate told herself as she woke up.

During breakfast she talked to Mr. Nordstrom. "Do you ever get extra honey?"

"Sometimes. In a good year. You look as though you have an idea."

Filled with excitement, Kate nodded. "If I help with the bees—"

Anders interrupted. "You want to be a *beekeeper*?"

Kate nodded, and shock registered in Anders' eyes. "Bees sting, you know."

"I know," answered Kate, her voice soft. "Are you afraid of them?"

"Of course not!" said Anders, his voice louder than it needed to be.

Looking up from her oatmeal, Kate caught the grin playing around Mr. Nordstrom's mouth. She tried not to smile as she asked, "What do you think?"

"Let's work together. I'll do the lifting and show you what to do. If we get a good crop—more than our family needs—you can take the extra jars to Grantsburg and sell them at the county fair."

"Great!" answered Kate. For the first time she dared to believe she might really get an organ.

As breakfast ended, Mama asked her to put away the milk. By now Kate knew what to do. Going outside, she set the pail of milk on the wooden platform surrounding the pump. As Kate opened a hinged trapdoor in the platform, she saw heavy timbers lining the walls of the well.

In the center of the well a pipe went up into the pump. Nearby hung a rope with a hook on the end. Lying down on her stomach, Kate grabbed the rope. Attaching the hook to the handle of the pail, she lowered the milk. Down next to the water it stayed cool, even in summer.

Just then Anders came up behind her. "Let's go," he said. "Time for school."

As Kate pushed herself up, the sleeve of her coat caught on a sliver of wood. Afraid it would tear, she lowered herself to free the material.

Anders hooted, then spoke in the quavery voice of an older woman. "In all my life—my wh-o-o-ole life—I never seen such a child for getting in trouble."

"Stop it!" said Kate, embarrassed again. Frantically she pulled at the wool thread wrapped around the splinter.

"But, child, how do you manage? One problem after another."

Then the thread came free, and Kate jumped up. A minute later she and Anders and Lars left for school.

This time Kate took no chances about having to find her way home. She noticed every step, every fork in the trail. Yet this morning Anders seemed different.

Maybe he'll be nice for a change. Kate was afraid to hope. Just the same, she decided to test it out. When Lars ran ahead out of earshot, she asked, "Do you know what I saw yesterday?" Soon she told Anders about the man digging down a box in the woods.

Anders looked puzzled. "Long curly hair, you say? And curly beard? Black?"

Kate nodded.

"Can't think of anyone around here who looks like that."

"But I saw him. I know I did!" answered Kate, afraid Anders wouldn't believe her.

"Can you remember anything else?"

"A black handlebar moustache," Kate answered. "Couldn't see his eyes very well, but I think they were blue." For a moment she thought. "No, maybe gray."

"Old clothes?"

Kate nodded. "Black. And dirty."

"Weren't you scared?"

For an instant Kate thought of lying, of saying, "Of course not!" the way Anders had at breakfast. But she wanted to be friends. She decided to risk it, and nodded, still afraid of what he'd say.

Anders was mean all right. "Well, it's good to know you're still a girl."

Kate almost hit him, but then caught the grin in his eyes—and the respect.

"Where's the box? Where's it buried?" Anders asked.

Lars was still ahead of them when they came to the cluster of birch and the big oak. Kate knelt down, swept the leaves and grass away, and showed Anders the spot. Anders' low whistle was all the thanks she needed.

"See the boot prints?" she asked. "They're crisscrossed from stamping, so it's hard to tell. But there's one clear print."

Anders knelt down for a closer look.

"There's something different about it," said Kate. "Is it a boot? Or a shoe? See the heel? The heavy outer line?"

"You're right," answered Anders. "And look at the toe. Almost as if there's an iron plate or something."

Then in the distance they heard the first bell ring.

"Have to go," said Anders. "I'm already in trouble with the teacher."

Quickly he replaced the leaves and grass. "Let's dig up the box after school. Maybe it's buried treasure. Maybe there'd be a reward, and I could buy a horse."

"Or an organ," answered Kate, then wished she could bite her tongue.

"An *organ*? Who wants an organ?"

"I do!" said Kate, sorry she'd let her secret slip out.

"But you can't ride an organ!"

"You're not supposed to, silly! You're supposed to play it!"

Anders began walking fast. As Kate hurried alongside, she caught his look. "Dumb girl!" it seemed to say. Right now, that's how Kate felt. *I wish I hadn't told him.*

As they entered school, Kate looked around and saw that the plain dress she wore today was more like those of the other girls. Yet her relief didn't last long. Soon after she sat down, she felt a slight tug on her braid.

Swinging around, she faced Erik Lundgren, the boy sitting behind her. Lifting his hands as if in surrender, his eyes widened with innocence.

"Stop it!" Kate said, so angry that she spoke aloud.

"I didn't do a thing!" he answered just as loud.

"Yes, you did! You stuck my braid in your inkwell." Kate was right. Pulling her long braid forward, she saw the end. Already the drying ink stiffened the hair.

Twisting her head, she pulled at her dress, trying to see the shoulders. Sure enough, splatters from the braid covered the material.

"Kate, what's the problem?" Miss Sundquist asked.

If I tell her, the boys will be even meaner. Kate ducked her head.

The boys snickered, but Anders gave them a look, and they stopped. As everyone went back to work, Kate felt grateful. She used a precious piece of paper to pass Anders a note.

Three people away from Kate, Miss Sundquist intercepted it. "Kate, this is a serious offense. I expect you to stay in for noon hour."

When lunch time came, the other children ate quickly, then hurried outside. For the first time in her life Kate felt glad to stay indoors. *At least I won't have another hour of trying to understand Swedish!*

Then she heard a ball bounce on the roof. "Anti-Over!" someone called. Kate knew the children must have chosen teams, lining up on opposite sides of the school building.

"Anti-Over!" came the call again. Kate was good at the game and wished she could join them. She reached the window in time to see Lars come around the schoolhouse and tag Anders.

That's strange. Anders is faster. He should have gotten away.

Anders wound up as if for a mighty toss. The ball sailed through the air. "Anti-Over!" he shouted.

Kate hurried to a window on the opposite side of the building. There the team waited, but no ball came over the roof. *Where'd it go?* But she didn't have time to find out.

"Kate!" called Miss Sundquist from her desk. Usually she went outside with the children. Today she remained at her desk, her half-eaten lunch in front of her.

"Yes, ma'am?"

"When I ask you to stay in, I expect you to stay in your seat."

Slowly Kate walked over and sat down. Picking up her book, she pretended to read. Then she heard the door open.

"Miss Sundquist?" asked Anders from the entryway.

"Yes, Anders?"

"The ball's caught in the bell tower. May I go up and get it?"

Miss Sundquist sighed. "All right. But be careful."

"Yes, ma'am. I will, ma'am."

As Kate waited, the sound of a ladder scraped the edge of the roof. Through a window she watched Anders' feet climbing the rungs. A minute later the ball rolled off the roof, landing outside a window. Anders scrambled down the ladder, and Kate went back to her reading.

Not long after, the game moved away from the school. Soon Kate wondered about the quiet. It seemed all the children had gone to the far end of the ball field.

"Kate, will you ring the bell, please?" asked Miss Sundquist.

Standing up, Kate felt grateful for the chance to move around. Going into the entryway, she grabbed the long rope that led to the bell and pulled.

Nothing happened. Kate tugged harder. Still no sound.

"What's the matter, Kate? Aren't you strong enough?"

"I'm fine, Miss Sundquist. I'll get it." This time Kate jumped high in the air, letting the whole weight of her body pull the rope.

But nothing happened. *That dumb Anders. It's one of his tricks.*

Coming out in the entryway, Miss Sundquist tried the rope. No sound came. "Go and call the children, Kate," she said.

Pulling on her coat, Kate went out, glad for the time outside. She was right. The children were all on the other side of the ball field.

When she reached them, Kate said, "Come on in."

A little girl looked at her, turned her hands palm up, then shrugged her shoulders.

Kate pointed to the school. "Miss Sundquist."

The little girl shrugged once more. Kate tried an older child, but couldn't understand the Swedish response.

Again Kate struggled to explain. Then an older boy laughed, and Kate caught on. Everyone was just pretending they didn't know what she said.

Quickly Kate turned away, not wanting them to see the hurt she felt. As she swung around, she bumped into Anders.

He'd been running, Kate could tell. His breath came in long gasps. Seeing him there, she felt angry all the way through. Knotting her fists, Kate beat them against his chest. "I hate you!" she stormed. "I hate you, hate you, hate you!"

For once Anders didn't fight back. Grabbing her hands, he stopped her. "Go on in," he whispered in English. "I'll tell you after school."

Turning to the children, Anders spoke in Swedish, and they obeyed him. Walking slowly, they started toward the schoolhouse.

12

Another Surprise

*W*ill the day ever be over? Kate felt impatient to talk with Anders. Minute by slow minute the afternoon dragged by.

As soon as Miss Sundquist let them go, Kate and Anders and Lars crossed the creek and started up the hill.

Anders poked along until Lars grew restless. "Beat you home!" Lars said, and Kate felt glad to see him run ahead.

"What was that all about?" she demanded.

"The school bell?" Anders grinned. "Well, it started out as a game. I threw the ball into the tower so I'd have an excuse to go up. Thought it was about time we had a longer lunch hour."

Kate laughed. "You managed that all right."

"Yup. There's a pulley hooked to the bell. I just took the rope out of the groove."

Then Anders' face grew serious. "Something else happened."

Though they seemed to be alone in the woods, he lowered his voice. "Turn around," he commanded.

They stood at the top of the steep hill behind the school, and Kate looked back.

"What do you see?" asked Anders.

"A good view of the school."

"Right. And what do you think you'd see if you were up in the bell tower?"

Kate thought for a moment. "A good view of this hill?"

"A *great* view of this hill," answered Anders. "And do you know who I saw on top of this hill?"

Kate couldn't guess.

"Your mysterious stranger!"

"Really? How do you know?"

"Baggy, dirty clothes. Curly black hair and beard. Handlebar moustache. Sound like him?"

Kate nodded, excitement bubbling up. "Sounds exactly like him."

"I tore up the hill as fast as I could," said Anders. "By the time I got here, he was gone. So I started down the path. I ran all the way back to where he buried the box. When I got there, nothing had changed. The leaves looked the way we left them."

"And the man?"

"I don't know. Maybe he heard me coming. Maybe he stepped back in the woods—" Anders didn't finish the sentence.

Kate said it for him. "Stepped back to hide. Maybe he's watching us now." She shivered.

Anders shook his head. "I don't think so. He heard me coming. He probably waited to see me leave. By now, he's probably gone."

"And the box?

"Let's go look," Anders said, his face grim.

Before long, Kate and Anders came to the clump of birch and the big oak. A heaped up pile of dirt and an empty hole marked the place where the box had been.

"It's gone!" Kate groaned. "The stranger didn't even bother to fill the hole!"

"Maybe he thought people would figure an animal did it. Does look kind of like a badger hole." Anders picked up a stick and poked it deep in the dirt. "Nothing here, all right."

Kate grabbed his sleeve. "Yes, there is." She pointed down at the soft dirt. "Look!"

Anders saw what she meant. "You're right! He's taken a branch and scratched out every print!"

Kate felt uneasy. "Sure acts as if he has a lot to hide. We better be careful."

Anders nodded, his blue eyes dark with thought.

After that, the week dragged by. On Saturday morning, as the sun peeked over the horizon, it wakened Kate. With relief she remembered she didn't have to go to school.

It felt good lying beneath the soft patchwork quilt. Stretching her arms high above her head, she looked over at Tina. The little girl was still sleeping. Her heart-shaped face looked soft and unprotected. Her white-blond hair spread out on the pillow.

They still weren't able to talk much together. During the week Kate had learned more Swedish and Tina more English. Yet after wanting a little sister for so long, it made Kate feel good just sharing a room with her. Tina seemed to like it too.

Trying to shut out the sun, Kate pulled the quilt over her head. She was almost asleep again when she heard what sounded like thunder. Boom! Boom! Boom!

Strange. How can it be thundering with the sun out?

Once again Kate heard the booms. This time her eyes flew open. "Gunshots!" she cried out.

Throwing back the covers, Kate leaped out of bed. "Sarah said it would be like this. She said it'd be wild in Wisconsin!"

Running back to the bed, she shook Tina's shoulder. "Wake up! Something's wrong!"

Boom! Boom! Boom!

Tina rolled over, and Kate shook her again. "There's a fight outside. We have to hide!"

Boom! Boom! The noise sounded closer. "Tina, how can you sleep through this?" Kate was desperate.

Tina opened one eye, then the other. As if in slow motion, she sat up, put her feet on the floor, then stood. Acting as though she had all the time in the world, she walked to the window near the big pine.

"Tina, have you lost your brains?" Kate felt frantic.

Tina motioned to her. "Look!" she seemed to be saying. Pushing up the window, she leaned out and pointed.

Through an opening between the branches, Kate saw the wagon track that passed the kitchen, granary, and chicken coop.

The back of the house blocked a full view, but Kate could see part of the pasture near the barn. This morning no cows grazed there.

Again, Tina pointed that way. Just then, another explosion rattled the windows. Boom! Boom! Two stumps flew high in the air.

Kate slid to the floor. "Will I ever get used to this place?" she asked, holding her head in her hands. She felt dumb, stupid, absolutely ridiculous. "What if Anders finds out?"

In that moment she remembered the little girl. "Tina, don't tell, will you?" Tina stood beside Kate, her face solemn, a question in her blue eyes. "You mustn't tell Anders or Lars," Kate repeated.

Then she remembered Tina didn't understand English. Putting her finger to her lips, Kate whispered, "Shhhhh! Shhhhh!" Next she pointed to herself, then outside.

This time Tina grinned. Pointing outside, then at Kate, she shook her head. They shared a secret now.

Kneeling on the floor beside Kate, Tina hugged her. Relief flooded Kate, and her arms went around her new sister.

As they dressed, Kate heard more booms, but they seemed farther away. When she and Tina went down, the rest of the family was at the breakfast table. Seeing the girls, Mama got their bacon and eggs from the warming oven of the cookstove.

Kate was full of questions. "What are you doing?" she asked Mr. Nordstrom.

"I've been using the field for pasture," he explained. "I want to get it ready for planting. So I drill a hole in each stump as deep as I can in the root system. Then I put in as many sticks of dynamite as I need."

"Why do the stumps keep blowing up, one after another?"

"I light a fuse in one stump, then go on to the next," he told her. "I have to move quickly, away from the one I've lit, so I don't get caught too close to the explosion."

When everyone finished eating, Mr. Nordstrom took down his big Bible. Together they read and prayed as they had every morning all week. Kate was beginning to like hearing the verses, but if someone had asked, she wouldn't have admitted it for anything.

Mr. Nordstrom pushed back his chair. "I want to make sure all the dynamite's exploded. Then I need help picking up. All of you except Ingrid." He smiled at Mama, and she smiled back, her eyes soft.

"Com'on, Kate," said Anders, his blue eyes teasing. "I'll show you how to get dirty."

Kate wrinkled her nose at him, remembering the first day of school.

She soon found Anders was right. Picking up blown-apart stumps was dirty work. Everyone pitched in, dragging the stumps to piles at different places around the field. Sometimes the pieces of wood were too big for Kate. Anders and his father took those, or left them to be blown apart again.

As the sun climbed higher, streaks of sweat started to mix with the dirt on Kate's body. Then she discovered all kinds of muscles she didn't know she had. Soon all she could think about was a soaking bath in the big washtub.

Yet all of them kept at it, even Tina. The piles of wood at different places around the pasture grew steadily higher. As Kate worked, she gradually moved to a far corner of the field, away from the house and barn, but next to the wagon track. From there the track wound through the trees to the dirt road leading to Grantsburg.

The sun was nearly overhead when she came to a stump that wasn't as shattered as the rest. A large portion still lay buried in the ground. Bending down to pick up a loose piece, Kate caught a glint of color. Bright red, it seemed.

Dropping to her knees, she began feeling around in the sandy soil. Brushing aside the dirt that spit up in the explosion, she uncovered what looked like red glass. Digging farther, she saw more red glass—one bead, then another. A moment later she pulled out a necklace.

"Hey, look!" she called, holding up her find. The glass glinted in the sunlight.

Tina was beside her immediately, her eyes shining through the dirt on her face.

Mr. Nordstrom looked puzzled. "Strange," he said. "What's a necklace doing under a stump?"

"Maybe there was a hollow place," answered Anders, his face just as dirty as Tina's. His blond hair looked gray. "Maybe there's more."

Lars was already down on his knees. "Where'd you find it?"

Kate showed them, and everyone began digging in the loose dirt around the stump.

Lars was the first to find another necklace, then Tina found one. All together they unearthed five necklaces—each of brightly colored glass.

"Where'd they come from?" asked Kate.

"I don't know." Mr. Nordstrom's eyes looked thoughtful. "We aren't far from Trader Carlson's. When he buys buckskin and furs from Indians, he trades them traps and food and things like this."

"But why would the necklaces be *here*?" asked Kate, the strangeness of it bothering her.

Lars's red hair was down in his face and his eyes were serious. "I seen them camp near here."

"Just the same, you've got something, Kate," said Mr. Nordstrom. "They always take their belongings with when they leave."

"And why would they hide *necklaces*?" asked Anders. One by one, he put the strings of beads across the palm of his hand, letting them hang down. The glass sparkled in the sunlight.

"Oh!" Kate gasped.

"What's wrong?" asked Lars.

Kate closed her mouth, trying to hide her surprise. "Oh, nothing." But something nagged at the back of her mind. Something she needed to remember.

Mr. Nordstrom's eyes looked thoughtful again. "Let's stop and eat. We'll show the beads to your mama and see if we can find the owner."

As they crossed the field, Kate dragged behind, trying to figure out what bothered her.

Anders dropped back to walk with her. "What is it?" he asked, his voice low so Tina wouldn't hear.

Kate turned to him. "If only I could remember." For a time she thought hard. "It's something to do with the sunlight. When you held up those beads . . ." Kate's voice trailed away. Walking on in silence, she racked her brain. "What is it about the sunlight?"

As they neared the farmhouse, something clicked in Kate's mind. "Remember a week ago?" she asked. "Last Saturday? My first day here?"

Anders grinned. Even through the dirt on his face, his blue eyes danced. "It's not hard to forget. The bull chased you."

For once Kate didn't bristle. "And I got so scared I forgot why I started across the field. Why I didn't see the bull."

Anders' grin faded, and his eyes grew serious.

Kate went on. "When I came out of the barn, I looked across to the trees on the other side of this pasture. I thought I saw something move. Then I figured I must be wrong. When I looked again, I saw a good climbing tree straight ahead. In the hollow where a branch goes out from the trunk, something glittered."

"Something like a necklace?"

Kate nodded, her eyes wide. "And something else. Something black. Something as tall as a man standing up. I thought it was a bear but. . . . What do you think?"

13

The Big Storm

*D*o I think it was a bear?" asked Anders. "I doubt it. But maybe—" Leaving the thought unfinished, he fell silent. Kate tried, but couldn't get him to tell what he thought.

As soon as they finished eating lunch, Kate and Anders hurried to the tree on the far side of the pasture. Anders pulled himself up to the lower branches and the hollow Kate remembered. But she wasn't surprised by what they found.

"It's empty!" Anders called down, as disappointed as Kate.

From that time on, both of them kept their eyes open for anything that seemed unusual. Wherever they went, they looked for the stranger. Yet one day followed the next without another glimpse of him. Mr. Nordstrom put the glass beads in a box and asked around, trying to find the owner.

The blustery days of March turned into April showers and then May flowers. Kate became better acquainted with some of girls at school. One of these was Josie Swenson.

Gradually Kate started to believe that Josie might become a real friend—a special friend, like Sarah Livingston.

Anders' pig grew, and the bees prospered. Mr. Nordstrom checked the hives often, and Kate helped him. By early May, when the maples budded, she knew how to direct smoke at the entrance and top, then quietly open a hive.

As the bees buzzed upward and their humming increased to a roar, Mr. Nordstrom stood nearby, watching to see if she could handle it. It took all of Kate's courage to stand still.

Then the bees swarmed around her, crawling up and down her overalls. "I'm not a scaredy-cat!" she told herself, remembering how Anders teased. "I'm not a scaredy-cat!"

When the bees lit on her arms and shoulders, it was even worse. Trying to push aside her fear of being stung, Kate took a deep breath, then let it out slowly. *I'll show Anders!* she thought, as she had many times before. Pushing the bellows of the smoker, she directed a cloud of smoke over her arms and legs.

"Good for you!" said Mr. Nordstrom, interrupting her thoughts. "See the pollen the bees are bringing in?"

As Kate watched, bees lit on the board in front of the hive entrance. Each carried lumps of pollen—tiny golden nuggets—in what Mr. Nordstrom said were baskets on their rear legs.

"Other worker bees put pollen in the honeycomb," he explained. "Here, I'll show you."

As he told Kate what to do, she lifted a frame from the center of the hive body.

"See how the bees pack away pollen?" he asked. "Look! There's the queen!"

A bee with a longer, larger body than the others moved across the frame. Immediately worker bees turned in her direction, clustering around.

"They always protect the queen," Mr. Nordstrom said. "If she died when there are no eggs in the hive, the other bees would gradually die out."

When Kate replaced the frame, Mr. Nordstrom showed her how to close the hive. "If this keeps on, we'll have a good year."

"With extra honey?" she asked.

A grin lit Mr. Nordstrom's sun-weathered face. "Yah, sure. If nothing goes wrong. Still want to buy an organ?"

Kate's heart jumped, glad he hadn't forgotten. "Yes, I want to buy an organ!" she exclaimed, thinking of all the songs she'd like to play. "Will there be enough money?"

Mr. Nordstrom shook his head. "But it'll be a start. You can put whatever money you earn in a jar, and add more when you can."

Walking to the house, Kate took off the straw hat and the thin curtain she used for a veil. "Maybe I can think up more ways to earn money," she said, pushing aside the hair that fell around her face. Getting an organ seemed even more of a possibility.

During the weeks that followed, Kate and Anders often talked about the mysterious stranger. "Why do we see him just once in a while?" asked Anders one morning the first week in June. "Why does he keep disappearing?"

Kate shook her head. They were out in the little house called a summer kitchen. Along one wall was the wood cookstove the family used during hot weather. Along another wall was a tall cupboard for storing dishes and pans. A shorter cupboard had a metal sink and pans for washing dishes. Anders sat on a bench near the third wall, leaning on the table.

Usually Kate liked it here. Today not even a whisper of breeze came through the open windows. The cookstove was still hot from breakfast, and Kate used it for ironing clothes. When one sadiron grew cool, she set it down on the stove. Detaching the handle, she reattached it to another, already heated iron. Licking her finger, she touched the bottom of the iron. It sizzled, and she knew it was hot enough.

"They're sure named right," she said. "Sadirons—makes me sad to use 'em." Running the iron across a piece of white cloth, she tested the heat before touching Tina's Sunday dress.

But Anders wanted to talk about the stranger. "Why doesn't anyone around here know him?" he asked, a frown creasing his tanned forehead.

"The stranger? No one knows him?"

"I asked Papa," said Anders. "He's never seen anyone who looks like what I said."

"Not anyone at all?"

"Nope, and Papa knows *everybody*. He warned me to be careful. To stay away from strangers and tell him if I see the man again."

"Did you tell him why you wondered?"

Anders nodded, his blue eyes puzzled. "Can you remember anything else?"

Kate shook her head, and the sweat on her forehead dripped into her eyes. As she thought about it, she finished ironing Tina's dress.

In the heat of June, that March day—her first day at Spirit Lake School—seemed far away. Recalling the woods and being lost in them, Kate felt a twinge of fear. Every so often the memory of her panic returned. Always she pushed that memory away, trying not to think about it. In the same way, she pushed aside the memory of her promise to God.

Now as Kate thought about standing on the large rock, watching the mysterious stranger, she recalled something. "He had a strange walk!" she exclaimed, setting down the iron to think about it.

"Strange?"

"As though his walk didn't fit his clothes."

Anders hooted. "Awww, Kate!"

Kate felt she had to defend herself. "I mean it!"

"His walk didn't fit his clothes?" Anders' blue eyes gleamed as though he wanted to laugh again. "Any other big clues?"

Kate bristled. "Maybe. Maybe not!"

"Hey, stop it! Don't be so pigheaded."

"Pigheaded, am I?" Kate was hot and tired, even though it was ten o'clock in the morning. "Big and fat like your old sow?"

Anders straightened his face. "Nah," he drawled. "Your eyes are prettier!"

Quickly Kate turned away, wondering if her face was as red as it felt.

"Come on, Kate. Don't be mad," pleaded Anders. "Do you remember anything else?"

Kate picked up another sadiron. "Wouldn't tell you if I did."

Anders shoulders slumped. He pushed back his chair and stood up. "Well!"

Kate felt as discouraged as he looked. She and Anders were taking care of the farm. Early that morning Mama and Mr. Nordstrom had driven off to Grantsburg for a new plow coming in on the Blueberry Special. It was a big day when someone went into town, and when they left Mama's eyes sparkled with excitement.

"Be sure you watch Lars and Tina," she reminded Kate before she left. "Take good care of them."

Now all Kate could think about was the heat. "Whew!" she said as Anders tapped the screen door to chase away the flies on the outside.

"Whew for sure," he answered. "It's hot!"

As the morning went on, the humidity grew steadily worse. Kate gave up on ironing. Yet when she moved away from the cookstove, the heat still felt as though it rose in waves from the ground.

The weather affected even Tina. Usually good-natured, the four-year-old was restless and out of sorts. Finally Kate found the Sears Roebuck catalogue. "If you promise to be very careful you can look at it."

By noon the air felt too heavy to breathe. In midafternoon clouds gathered along the horizon.

As the faraway rumbles of thunder moved closer, Kate sought out Anders in the barn. "Anders? What do you do if there's a real bad storm?"

For once Anders didn't call her scaredy-cat. Instead, he went outside and looked at the sky. In the southwest lightning shattered the blackness. Thunder rumbled. Around Kate and Anders not a leaf moved.

As they watched, the clouds grew larger. "Where are Tina and Lars?" he asked.

"In the house looking at the wish book."

"Let's not say anything yet," he answered. "No use scaring 'em. But I'll get the cows in."

He whistled between his teeth, and Lutfisk bounded around the corner of the barn. Anders raised his right arm high and pointed in the direction of the pasture. "Go get 'em," he ordered, and Lutfisk took off.

"The cows will know it's early and won't want to come. I better help him."

As he started to follow Lutfisk, Kate stopped Anders with

her question. "Where do you go if it's really bad?" she asked
again.

"The root cellar, Papa said once. But don't worry. We've never
had to use it. Just keep an eye on Tina and Lars."

Kate returned to the house but kept looking out the windows.
Finally she went back outside. As she stood on the edge of the
steep hill, she had a good view across Rice Lake. The sky looked
angry. A large fan-shaped cloud gathered in the southwest.

Moment by moment, the rumble of thunder moved closer.
With it Kate's tension grew. Faraway lightning flashed pink in
the dark clouds.

She wished Anders would come.

Then she remembered Mama and Mr. Nordstrom. *Where are
they? Still in Grantsburg? Or on the way home?* In that moment
she recalled every story she'd heard about wagons and buggies
struck by lightning.

Trying to push those thoughts aside, Kate hurried back to
the house. Yet her worry wouldn't go away. *What if they get
caught out in the open? What if they can't get to shelter?*

Up until now she'd often worried about Mama. Often she'd
thought, *What would I do without her?* Now it felt strange having
someone else to be scared about. It surprised Kate to realize she
cared about what happened to Mr. Nordstrom.

The next time Kate went outside to look at the sky, Tina followed. Once more the sky had changed. The clouds were no
longer black, but green. Like water in a kettle, they seemed to
boil. The air felt still and heavy.

"Tina, go to the root cellar," Kate ordered, running for the
house. "Lars! Come on!"

The root cellar was a small room dug into the side of the hill
between the summer kitchen and the barn. As Lars caught up
to Tina, he ran ahead and pulled open the door. Inside was a
short passageway, then a second door leading into a dark, hole-
like room. Shelves for storing food lined three walls. Under
them, bushel baskets waited for a new crop of potatoes.

Now before harvest the shelves were almost empty, and Kate
stacked baskets to make room to sit down. Tina and Lars
dropped to the dirt floor, while Kate hurried back outside.

Mama's picture! Running to the house, she snatched it up, then rushed back to the root cellar. Carefully she set the picture on a top shelf. Then, as soon as she caught her breath, she returned outside.

"Where's Anders?" she worried aloud.

Lars followed her. "Should I look for him?"

"You better wait here," said Kate. "He's getting the cows. I'm sure he'll come."

The lightning seemed closer now, the clouds greener. Then Kate heard Lutfisk bark. "Anders must be on the other side of the barn."

It seemed forever before he came out on Kate's side. A sudden gust of wind caught the barn door, swinging it back to crash against the building. Anders grabbed it, flung it shut, and dropped the bar that held the door in place.

Trees bent low before the wind. Nearby, a branch broke off and sailed through the air. "We're here!" shouted Kate, but the wind brought the words back to her.

Anders headed for the house, and Kate called again. "Over here!"

This time Anders heard and changed direction. Bending low, he struggled against the wind, Lutfisk tagging behind.

Lars headed back into the cellar, and Kate followed. Just as Anders reached the outer door, a mighty thud shook the earth. Anders tumbled into the passageway.

"Take the dog!" Pushing Lutfisk in, Anders grabbed the outer door. The wind flung it back, but with a mighty heave, Anders managed to close it, then the inner door.

Still short of breath from running, he dropped to the dirt floor.

"What was that?" asked Kate.

"The crash? Probably a tree," he answered.

In the darkness Tina started to cry.

14

Discovery!

"I want Mama," whimpered Tina from the blackness of the cellar. By now Kate knew enough Swedish to understand.

"I do too," she answered. In the dark she felt Tina's hand reaching out for hers. Pulling the little girl onto her lap, Kate gave her a hug.

"I wish Papa was here," said Lars, his voice small and scared.

"I wish *both* of them were here," Anders chimed in. Always Anders acted so sure of himself, as if he didn't need anyone. But not now.

Me too. Kate felt afraid to say it aloud. She wondered if Mama and Papa were safe. Had they found shelter somewhere? More than that, Kate wished all of them were together. The idea surprised her.

Then she realized something else. Before this, when alone, she'd practiced calling Mr. Nordstrom *Papa.* But never before had she called him Papa in her thoughts.

When did Anders and Lars and Tina start calling Mama by that name? Somewhere along the way it just happened. *Is that what Mama meant when she said, "As Mr. Nordstrom and I help each other, we'll grow to love one another"*?

Now a movement in the darkness startled Kate. "What's that?"

"It's me," said Anders. "Should be some candles somewhere." For a time he searched the shelves, feeling his way. Finally he had to give up.

Just then another thud shook the earth. "That was close," said Anders. "Must be the big oak back of the house."

Now and then the wind whistled through a crack in the outer door. As the rain beat against it, Kate felt scared again. "Where do you think they are?" she asked.

"Mama and Papa? They're inside somewhere." But Anders' voice lacked its usual confidence. "Papa's good about weather," he went on, as though talking himself into believing they were all right. "Being a farmer, he has to be. He notices things."

As they waited, the darkness seemed to close in around Kate. Her scared feelings changed to panic. Then she remembered another day, three months before—the day she was lost in the woods.

She had cried out to God, making a promise. "If you help me, I'll believe you can take care of me. I'll even believe you do good things!"

But now Kate felt ashamed. *The minute I was safe, I forgot about you, God. I figured I did it on my own.*

For a time the cellar was quiet except for the dog's panting. Still hugging Tina with one arm, Kate reached out with her other hand. Feeling the hair on the dog's back, she moved her hand forward and scratched behind his ears. When Lutfisk turned his head to lick her hand, Kate was surprised. Always Lutfisk had been Anders' dog.

The minutes stretched long in the quiet cellar. *I'm your bad-weather friend, God. When I'm scared, I ask for help. When I'm all right, I forget about you. How would I feel if Sarah was my friend only when she needed help?*

Tina moved in her arms, and Kate wondered if the darkness bothered Tina as much as the storm. When the little girl drew a long shuddering breath, Kate began to hum, low and soft. Long ago, Daddy had sung whenever she was scared. Now Kate hummed a lullaby she'd learned from him.

Then she had a terrible thought. *What if Anders laughs?* In the middle of the song she stopped.

A moment later Tina started singing. In a clear, high voice she sang words Kate didn't understand.

"What's she singing?" Kate asked softly.

From the darkness Lars spoke just as quietly. "A Swede song, 'Children of the Heavenly Father.' "

Anders remained silent, but Tina kept singing. Strangely enough, Kate felt better, even though she didn't understand the words. She felt the change in the musty cellar.

Then as suddenly as it started, the rain stopped beating at the outer door. In the darkness Kate heard Anders crawl toward the entrance. "It's moved on. The storm's passed."

One by one they left the shelter—Lars, Tina, then Kate. Outside, she looked around, shocked by what she saw.

A short distance from the root cellar a huge oak lay on the ground, leaving a gaping hollow where the roots had been. The long trunk stretched across the yard, its sprawling branches barely missing the house.

Anders walked over and stood beside the tree. In spite of his height, the upended roots towered above him. Slowly he turned, looking toward the house, the barn, the granary, and the summer kitchen. Here and there, shingles had blown off, but all the buildings stood.

As if in a dream, Anders moved to the front of the house. The others followed. There they found three more uprooted trees. Once again the branches reached out, stretching long across the grass. Yet they had fallen away from the house.

For the first time since Kate had known Anders, he looked visibly shaken. Watching him, her scared feeling returned and with it a gnawing at the pit of her stomach. When Tina took her hand, Kate felt glad she could hang on to something.

For a long moment the children stood there. All around lay large and small branches, tossed about by the wind. Leaves littered the grass.

Kate looked beyond the house to the woods. Even at this distance she could see the wind's path through the trees. "I can't believe it! How could the house stand through all this?"

"Even the windows didn't break!" said Anders, speaking for the first time since they left the cellar.

Then Kate saw the beehives. Standing at the edge of the hill, they'd caught the full force of the wind. Toppled over, the hive bodies lay on their sides.

"Our honey!" Kate exclaimed, running forward.

As she moved closer, the bees swarmed upward, buzzing angrily. Quickly she stepped back.

Usually the hive bodies held the frames apart, giving the bees room to move between. Now, the frames spilled out on the ground, crushing and holding the bees.

"All our work for nothing!" groaned Kate, feeling sick.

"What do you mean?" asked Anders, coming to stand beside her.

"A queen usually stays in the center of a hive. The frames are so squashed together the queen in each hive might be dead. No wonder the bees are mad!"

"They're mad all right. Look at 'em!" Anders edged back.

Just then a spatter of raindrops touched Kate's face. She looked at the sky. "I have to get 'em back."

"Back? Back together?"

"See that cloud? It's going to rain again. Soon it'll be dark."

"Kate, those bees are *mad*."

"Wouldn't you be, too, if your house was blown apart?"

"You're going to fix 'em? You're crazy!"

Kate's chin shot up. "And you, Anders Nordstrom, are going to help me."

"You are crazy! I'm not getting near those bees!"

"If we don't get the hives together, we might lose the whole honey crop."

"So? Do it yourself then."

"I can't. They're too heavy."

Anders started to walk away.

Kate shouted after him. "Anders, it's the beginning of June! The most important time of the year!"

"For what?" Anders shouted back, his voice defiant.

"For building up the hives—so there're lots of bees for making honey."

"So?" he asked again.

"So you won't have honey on your bread all year. So Mama won't have honey for baking. And if we don't have honey to sell, I'll never get an organ!" Kate's voice ended in a wail.

Anders groaned, but he turned back. "All right, all right. What do I do?"

"Find your papa's hat and veil."

Quickly Kate put on the old pair of overalls, and she and Anders tied string around their ankles. When Kate put on gloves and draped the curtain around her straw hat, Anders laughed at the way she looked.

But he didn't laugh long. As soon as Kate had the smoker working, they moved quietly toward the first hive. The bees rose around Kate, and she blew smoke at them. When they quieted a bit, she took the bottom board and set it on the log platform that held the hive off the ground. Then she told Anders, "All right, help me lift."

With Anders carrying most of the weight, they set a hive body on the bottom board. Kate spaced out the frames. Then they set a second and a third box on top of the first. As quickly as she could, Kate replaced the cover and went on to the next hive.

Once she glanced at Anders. His whole body looked stiff, as though waiting for a thousand stings. Even his eyes seemed scared. Yet instead of running, he stood there.

Together they finished the second hive. As Kate moved toward the third, she saw something shiny between the logs of the platform. Getting down on her knees, she took a closer look, reached in, and pulled something out.

"Kate, hurry up!"

"Just a minute!" A square piece of copper lay in Kate's glove. As she turned it over, several bees settled on her arm. A stinger went through her sleeve, and Kate jumped.

"Com'on, Kate, let's get outta here!"

Kate stuffed the copper piece in a pocket of her overalls and picked up the smoker. As she pushed the bellows, clouds of smoke billowed over the bees and frames still on the ground. Yet the angry bees didn't let her alone. This time a stinger reached her shoulder.

Kate flinched and tried to hold down her panic. All she wanted was to get out of there. As quickly as they could, she and Anders put the third hive together.

"We did it!" she exclaimed on the way to the house. As soon as she could, she'd get mud on her stings.

Walking quickly but not running, Anders hurried away from the bees. At a safe distance he stopped and pulled off his veil. "What did you find back there?"

Pulling the curtain from her hat, Kate took the copper piece from her pocket. As Anders turned it over, he gave a long, amazed whistle. "Kate, look at this!"

Thunder rumbled, and Kate knew that rain would return. But Anders didn't seem to care. In the fading light of the day he turned over a piece of copper about four inches square and a quarter of an inch thick. "Look, Kate!" he exclaimed again.

Leaning closer, she saw the letters stamped on one side. "S-v-e-r-i-g-e," she spelled out. "Sweden?"

"Yup!" exclaimed Anders. "It's a genuine stamp of the crown of Sweden. It must be very old."

"And valuable?"

Anders nodded. "Probably. At least to the owner." His eyes gleamed. "Maybe he'd give a reward."

"A big one?"

Anders shrugged. "Who knows? It sure is worth *something*!"

"Enough to buy an organ?"

Anders shook his head. "Nope. Enough to buy a horse."

"An organ."

"A horse."

Kate felt the flush of anger move up into her cheeks. Her long black braid flipped around her shoulders. "An organ."

"A horse," he said firmly.

Kate stomped her foot. "I found it. An organ."

"You wouldn't have found it if I hadn't helped you."

Now Kate was really angry. "You— You—" she sputtered. "A horse."

Then Kate caught the teasing in his blue eyes. She sighed. "You are *mean*."

Anders grinned. "Yah, sure." He sounded like Papa.

For the first time all day Kate laughed. Anders joined her, and Kate laughed again. All the tension she'd felt as she watched the storm build up drained out of her. Kate wondered if Anders sensed the relief she felt.

Then she remembered. "Mama and Papa? Do you think they're all right?"

As Anders nodded, Kate realized it was the first time she'd called Mr. Nordstrom *Papa* outloud. *Will Anders notice? I don't want to be teased.* If he did, Anders didn't say anything.

"Do you *really* think they're all right?" Kate asked again, now when Tina and Lars couldn't hear.

For once Anders looked solemn. "Yup," he answered. "I can't explain it. Sometimes when Papa leaves me in charge I think, 'Can I do it?' I wonder if I can do even little things. But now—" He broke off, unwilling or unable to say what he was feeling.

In a moment he spoke again as though to reassure Kate. "It'll take longer because of the storm."

Kate looked around. The huge oaks lay on the ground, their roots high in the air. It would take days to clean up the leaves and broken branches. But somehow she felt better.

Anders grinned, as though he couldn't stay serious too long. "Well then, you better get supper ready."

Kate imitated his tone. "Well then, you better get the cows milked."

Then she remembered the copper piece Anders still held in his hand. "What should we do with it?"

"We better hide it."

"But where? It's so strange, all the things happening around here. Where would it be safe?"

Anders looked thoughtful. "Maybe we should set a trap."

15

Missing!

$\mathcal{A}$ trap?" asked Kate.

"Let's use the copper piece to find out who put it there. Maybe it's the man we saw in the woods."

"Good idea!"

"Glad you like it," Anders drawled. "It's your job to put the piece back."

"Mine?" Kate remembered how angry the bees had been. The stings on her arm and shoulder itched and burned. She knew they'd get worse.

"Yup. Since you like bees so much. And let's keep a lookout tonight. Your bedroom has the best view of the hives, but I can see them too."

They agreed that Kate would watch the first half of the night, Anders the second.

"We should have a signal," Kate said.

"If you need me, rap on the wall between the bedrooms." As they reached the house, Anders knocked on the siding. "A long, steady rap to say, 'Your turn. Take over.' I'll rap back the same way so you know I'm awake."

"What if I need help?"

"One long rap. Wait a second or two. Two short ones. Keep repeating it 'til I hear."

A moment later, Tina tugged at Kate's hand. Kate knew the little girl was hungry. Going into the summer kitchen, she lit the kerosene lamp, glad for the glow it shed in the growing darkness.

Gathering kindling, Kate started a fire in the cookstove. Then, slipping back outside, she pushed the copper piece into the hollow space beneath the third hive. By the time Anders finished milking, Kate had soup and hot biscuits ready.

During supper it rained again, but the fury of the earlier wind was gone. When Tina grew sleepy, Kate led her into the house and tucked her into bed. Taking a quilt and pillow, Kate sat down by the window, leaning against the sill to watch.

A gentle breeze touched her there. As the clouds blew away, the moon came up, and Kate felt grateful. If Mama and Papa were trying to get home, the light would help them.

From here Kate had a clear view of the wagon track as it passed the side of the house and curved around the front. Near the beehives, rainwater filled a deep rut. The water shimmered in the moonlight.

Roads must be awful again. Kate remembered their trip from Grantsburg in the March mud. *Will they get through? Where are they?*

As Kate watched, the shadows of bushes near the hives wavered in the breeze. Now and then the moon went under a cloud, then reappeared, seeming brighter than ever. Once the bushes moved more than usual, and Kate sat up. *What's that?*

Crouching by the window, she almost stood up to rap for Anders' help. Then an animal moved away from the bushes. A black animal with a white stripe down its back. Kate relaxed, once more leaning against the window. Only three months before, she would have hidden under the quilt until the skunk passed. By now she'd seen them often and knew she was far enough away.

As Kate watched, the skunk waddled across the pasture. From inside the house Lutfisk woofed. *Would he be just as good a watchdog if a man came to the hive?*

Kate's eyelids grew heavy. The events of the day seemed to march like a parade in front of her. Down in the root cellar they had seemed like a family with all the children together.

Kate yawned. As a shadow darker than night moved toward the hive, she rubbed her eyes. Lutfisk barked again, but Kate barely heard. Putting her head on the windowsill, she fell into an exhausted sleep.

———

Morning sunlight wakened Kate. She was still sitting by the window, fully dressed. *What am I doing here?*

Then she saw the uprooted trees sprawled around the house and remembered the storm. When she recalled the copper piece, she jerked upright. *Did anything happen when I was asleep?*

In the double bed Tina sprawled spread-eagle, sound asleep. Slipping quietly out of the room, Kate went downstairs. The first floor was as empty as she feared. Mama and Papa weren't home.

"The roads are muddy," Kate told herself firmly. Yet she knew they were long overdue, and her stomach muscles tightened.

In the summer kitchen, she started a fire in the cookstove, then went to the well. Lifting the trapdoor, she lay down on the platform and tugged at the rope. Hand over hand she pulled up the pail of milk. As she tried to stand up, her dress caught on the sliver of wood. Carefully she freed herself, then hurried back to make breakfast.

First Lars, then Tina found her there. Kate was almost ready with pancakes when Anders came in from milking, his broad shoulders slumped.

As he dropped into a chair, Anders looked more tired than Kate had ever seen him. But Kate guessed that something else bothered him. Even with muddy roads, Mama and Papa should have been home. If it weren't for Lars and Tina, she would have asked, "Are you *sure* they're all right?" Instead, Kate swallowed her questions.

Breakfast was even quieter than last night's supper. For the first time since Kate had known him, Anders pushed pancakes around on his plate.

When they finished eating, Anders stood up and took the big Bible down from the shelf. Looking uncomfortable, he glanced at Kate as though hoping she wouldn't make a smart remark. Kate stared, so surprised that she couldn't think of one.

Anders turned to the psalm Papa had read on Kate's first day at the farm. "God *is* our refuge and strength, a very present help in trouble."

His voice grew stronger. "Therefore will not we fear. . . ."

When he finished, Anders closed the Bible. Looking even more uncomfortable, he bowed his head and closed his eyes.

As Kate stared, she caught Tina watching her. Kate bowed her head and peeked when Tina wasn't looking.

When Anders prayed, his words came in a rush. "Jesus, wherever Mama and Papa are, we ask you to take care of them. We ask that you bring them home safely. Ah-men."

Still not looking at Kate, Anders pushed back from the table, his chair scraping on the wood floor. As he stood up, he straightened his broad shoulders as though taking on the world.

A moment later Kate heard the sound—a wagon coming up the hill. Running outside, she saw Dolly and Florie come around the barn. "They're here!" Kate shouted. "They're home!"

Papa stopped the horses and jumped down. As Mama reached the ground, she turned to Kate. When Kate felt Mama's arms go around her, the tears she'd been holding back spilled over.

Mama let her cry. As Kate's sobs quieted, she stood back. Mama held Kate at arms' length, looking into her eyes. Mama's cheeks also were wet with tears.

At last Kate looked at Mr. Nordstrom. He was trying to hug everyone at once—Anders, Lars, and Tina. His long arms almost went around all of them.

As Kate watched, she wanted to tell him how glad she was that he was safe, how good it was to have him home. But suddenly she felt shy before this man she now called Papa in her thoughts.

She hung back, and her tongue felt tied to the roof of her mouth. When Mr. Nordstrom turned to her, holding open his arms, Kate turned away.

Only then did Mr. Nordstrom notice the uprooted trees. "Looks like we've got some work cut out for us, Anders."

Anders grinned. "Well, it's wood for winter." The relief that

Papa was home shone in his eyes.

The Blueberry Special had been delayed, Mama and Papa told them. It was late afternoon before trainmen unloaded the new plow. By then the sky was dark and green. Papa put the horses in a livery stable, and he and Mama went to the Antler's Hotel to wait. At six o'clock the storm hit Grantsburg.

"North of here it's really bad," said Papa. "Probably was a cyclone. Fallen trees blocked the road in several places."

"Coming home it was too dark to see," said Mama. "But there must be a number of houses and barns destroyed."

It was late afternoon before Kate had time to check for the copper piece. Putting on her overalls, gloves, and veil, she crossed the muddy wagon track. Kneeling down on the back side of the third hive, away from the entrance, she reached into the hollow.

Her glove came up empty.

Did I push it back farther than I thought? She tried to ignore a sick feeling. Pulling off her glove, she felt with her hand.

Still finding nothing, she squinted under the platform. Unable to see the copper piece, she stretched out on her stomach, her fingers feeling back as far as she could reach.

A bee buzzed up and circled her head, humming angrily. More bees followed, and Kate puffed smoke in their direction. When several lit on her shoulders and arms, she aimed the smoker toward herself. But the bees were still upset from the day before. Finally, Kate gave up and headed for the house.

Near the wagon track, she met Anders, and had to tell him. "It's gone! The copper piece is missing!"

"Gone! But you watched last night. You didn't see the stranger, did you?"

Kate was embarrassed to tell him. "I fell asleep."

For once Anders didn't tease her. "Well, to tell the truth, so did I. That's why I didn't hear whether you rapped for me."

"I missed our big chance," moaned Kate, her shoulders slumping. "Up 'til now, everything's been hidden away from the house. This was close enough to watch."

Together they started back across the wagon track. Horseshoe prints and the wheels of the returning wagon marked the mud. Yet as they walked to the other side, Kate noticed something. "Anders! Look at this!"

Near the edge of the track Kate knelt down. In spite of the wagon and horses, there was one clear print. "That's it!"

"That's what?" asked Anders.

"The print we saw in the woods. From a boot or shoe. The print left by the mysterious stranger!"

"Aha!" Anders knelt down for a better look. "Yup! Same funny outline. The heavy outer line around the heel."

"Around the toe too," said Kate. "Maybe it's the iron plate you talked about."

Then Kate thought of something that troubled her. "Anders? That day with the dynamite? When I wondered if I'd seen a bear?"

Anders stood up, and Kate stood with him. "You didn't really think that, did you?" she asked.

She was looking into his eyes now, and Kate knew he wouldn't lie to her. "Did you think it was the stranger instead?"

Slowly Anders nodded. "I didn't want to scare you. It's always been safe living out here. No one has ever bothered us."

Kate felt scared all right. "And he's coming closer to the house." A tingle ran down her spine.

Anders started across the grass. "Something still bothers me. We know the stranger's around here some place. But why's he here just now and then? Why does he come around, then disappear?"

16

County Fair

*T*wo days later, Lars ran all the way from the mailbox. "It's here!" he shouted, bringing in the June 8th *Journal of Burnett County*. The family gathered around to read the first newspaper report of the storm.

A week later, the paper included a more complete description of injuries and damage in the area. Not until the June 22nd issue did the *Journal* print pictures and the full story.

Passing north of Windy Hill Farm, the cyclone had left a wide swath of destruction on either side of its path. Miraculously no one was killed.

Since the day of the storm, something had changed inside Kate. Whenever she was with Mr. Nordstrom, she still avoided speaking to him by name. In her thoughts it was a different matter. While she continued to call her Irish father *Daddy*, she increasingly thought of Mr. Nordstrom as *Papa*.

During the weeks that followed, she and Anders did not catch even a hint that the stranger might be somewhere about. Yet both of them kept thinking about the man and his mysterious appearances. Whenever Kate noticed soft earth, she looked for the strange boot print. "What is it that made that print different?" she asked Anders more than once.

Then, on another warm day when Tina was looking through the Sears Roebuck catalogue, Kate thought of something.

"Tina, let me see the wish book for a minute, all right?" Taking the catalogue, Kate turned to the section on men's shoes. Tina grew restless as Kate read the description of one shoe after another. At last she found what she was looking for.

Clutching the catalogue, Kate sought out Anders. "Look!" she exclaimed, her excitement spilling over. "Read this!"

MEN'S MINING SHOE, $1.50. At an additional cost we have fitted this shoe with a heavy iron toeplate, and also encircled the heel with a heavy iron plate, thereby making it practically indestructible.

Anders whooped. "That's it, all right! The kind of shoe that'd make the print we saw!" Then his excitement dimmed. "But there's no mining around here. Who would wear a miner's shoe?"

When they asked Papa Nordstrom about it, he agreed. "You're right. Years ago there was talk of a copper mine in Trade Lake. But it didn't work out. Can't think of anyone who'd wear that kind of shoe."

Much as they wanted to know more, Kate and Anders could not find further clues.

As summer slipped by, Anders brushed his pig each morning, getting it ready for the county fair. Rosie had fattened up nicely, and Anders had high hopes of winning a blue ribbon.

On a hot day in August Papa Nordstrom decided how much honey the bees needed for winter. He and Kate removed the rest of the honey from the hives. It was hard work taking off the top boxes called supers and brushing the bees off the frames.

Using a knife heated in hot water, Mama removed the layer of wax that capped the combs. Then Papa put the frames in an extractor, and spun out the honey. Kate and Mama poured it into jars and pails.

"Do we have enough?" Kate asked.

"Enough for what?" Papa answered, as though he didn't remember what she meant.

"You know." Then she caught his grin. "We do, don't we?"

"Yah, enough to sell some," he promised. "Not enough for an organ, but a start."

"Great!" Kate exclaimed. The bee stings she'd received didn't seem important anymore.

At last the Saturday of the Burnett County Fair arrived. Anders blocked off the back part of the farm wagon. Papa helped him get the squealing pig inside.

In the middle part of the wagon Papa and Anders set wooden boxes packed with jars of honey for the street fair. People from miles around would bring whatever they wanted to sell.

It was still dark when Papa clucked the horses, and they started down the hill. Mama and Anders were up beside Papa. The rest sat in the wagon bed behind.

Kate watched Mama talk and laugh. *She's different now. Happier, I guess. She even sings around the house, the way she did when Daddy was alive.*

As they turned onto the road for Grantsburg, another thought surprised Kate. *I haven't been lonesome for Sarah and Michael for a long time.*

With the hot winds of summer the road was dry, and the trip went well. When the family reached the Grantsburg fairgrounds, Anders and Papa unloaded the pig while Lars went for a bucket of water. Then Anders washed Rosie and started the careful grooming needed for a blue ribbon.

Around Kate, clusters of people formed. As she listened, men and women who lived far out in the country greeted friends they hadn't seen for a time.

Papa found an empty place along the street and set up sawhorses and boards for a table. Kate covered the boards with a cloth, then set out the honey. Golden and clear in the sunlight, it looked mouth-watering.

Before long, the first buyer came by. As Kate tucked the money away, she felt excited. Soon another woman stopped, put down her money, and set the jar in her market basket. By noon there were only five jars left.

Kate's excitement mounted as she remembered Papa's words: "Every bit helps!" Her little purse was growing fat.

Then a young couple came to the table. *They're not much*

older than me, Kate thought. After asking the price, the husband
and wife walked a short distance away to talk.

"It's just what we need," the girl said. "If we're careful, five
jars will take us through winter."

Kate could barely hear the man's answer. "For *all* your cook-
ing and bread baking?"

The girl nodded. "I'll use the smallest amount I can."

Her husband sighed. "I don't know what to do. If the storm
hadn't wiped out everything, we'd have something to sell too."

"But when we don't have much else to eat . . ."

The young man nodded. "Yah, you're right." He reached
deep into his pocket and pulled out a flat leather coin purse.
"You get the honey. I'll help you carry it to the wagon."

As they headed back to the table, Kate turned away, pretending she hadn't heard. Swallowing a lump in her throat, she
tried to push aside a feeling she used to know well.

Before Mama married Papa Nordstrom, Kate had known that
feeling often. It came whenever Kate heard Mama cry at night.
It came when Kate wondered if there'd be enough money for
food. Always that empty feeling gnawed at the pit of her stomach.

"We'd like all five jars," the girl said in a quiet voice. As she
held up two cloth bags, her husband put the money on the table.

"Just a minute," said Kate. "I'll pack 'em so they don't break
on your way home." Kneeling down, she collected newspaper
from a box they'd used for the honey.

Once again Kate thought about the long winter after Daddy
died. Often she'd gone to bed feeling hungry and scared.

I want an organ. With all my heart I want an organ. But deep
inside Kate knew the truth. *I don't have to have it.*

Then the idea struck her. With one hand Kate gave the young
wife some newspaper. With the other, she picked up the money.
As she knelt behind the table for more paper, she pulled out her
handkerchief. Quickly she put the coins inside and tied a knot.

Holding the handkerchief in her hand, Kate reached for the
last jar of honey. Kneeling once more, she set the handkerchief
on the lid and wrapped paper around the money and jar. Standing up again, she set the jar in one of the girl's bags.

"Looks like you're all sold out," said the young man.

Kate nodded. "Thanks for your business. Hope you like the honey."

"We will," replied the girl. Each of them picked up a bag. Soon they were lost in the crowd.

The minute they were gone, Kate felt sorry about what she'd done. *How could I have been so stupid? Giving away five jars?*

Then she had an even worse thought. *Maybe they planned that I heard them.*

Like a mouse finding cheese, the awful thought nibbled away in Kate's mind. Finally she pushed the idea from her, refusing to think about it. *No! They were honest.*

Folding up the cloth, Kate took down the boards and set them against a tree. After stacking the boxes, she decided to look around.

Walking slowly, Kate started down the block, stopping now and then to see what people offered for sale. She was almost ready to turn around when she came to a corner. There she stopped, startled by what she saw.

Set back, away from the street and the dust, was an organ. A reed pump organ. Just the kind of organ Kate dreamed about buying!

17

Scaredy-cat?

*A*s Kate stood there, she forgot everything around her. A reed organ! The pipe organ in Minneapolis had to be pumped by someone else. Yet Kate could play this one by herself. She'd just pump the foot pedals up and down.

It's the most wonderful organ in the world! Beautiful carving decorated the high wooden back. On either side of the music rack were small shelves for kerosene lamps. Next to the keyboard were ten stops for changing the sound being played.

Kate moved closer for a better look. The ivory keys looked new, as though they'd never been used.

The owner of the organ walked forward. "Want to try it, young lady?"

Would I! Kate thought. But she felt shy, trying to play in front of someone else.

"Ah, come on," encouraged the man. "Have you had lessons?"

Kate shook her head.

"Why don't you try it anyway?"

Why not? With everyone milling around, maybe no one would notice.

As Kate sat down on the organ stool, her heart leaped into

116

her throat. Placing her feet on the pedals, she began to pump and heard the soft whoosh of air coming in.

The man reached over and pulled out a few stops. "Now give it a try."

Kate set her fingers on the keyboard, the way she'd seen organists do. The chords sounded mixed up and strange. Moving her fingers around, she listened until the notes blended. Then, using only her right hand, Kate picked out a tune.

Before long she forgot the man standing near the organ, the people passing by on the street. When she felt sure of the melody, she added chords with her left hand, changing the notes until they fit.

Then the special tunes Kate had played in her mind seemed to leap into her fingers. Excitement welled up within her. She couldn't explain it, even to herself. Yet she could play, even though she had never been taught!

At last Kate stopped, not wanting to, but suddenly feeling self-conscious. Standing up, she asked, "How much does it cost?"

"It's a real good organ," he answered. "New in 1885. Solid oak cabinet. Not a nick on it. Everything in perfect—"

"How much?" Kate interrupted.

"I'll sell it to you for twenty dollars. That's a real bargain."

"Fifteen."

"Nineteen."

"Fifteen fifty."

The man shook his head.

"If you have to take it home again—"

"Still have half a day to sell it."

But then Kate remembered. Even if he sold it for sixteen dollars, she didn't have half that much. "I'll talk to my papa," she said in a small voice.

Feeling surprised she had called him that, Kate started away, then turned back. For a long moment she looked at the organ, then started out once more.

This time she almost bumped into Papa Nordstrom. Seeing him there with Anders, Kate felt embarrassed. *Did they hear me play?*

Then she had an even worse thought. *Did they hear me bargain with the man? I don't want Anders to tease me.*

"You're a good organ player, Kate," said Papa gently.

Kate swallowed hard and looked at the ground. He had heard, all right. All of it.

Then she remembered the money. Digging deep in her purse, Kate pulled out the coins she'd earned selling honey. Papa opened his hands, and she dropped the money into them. Once more she felt sorry she'd given five jars away.

At the same time, Anders took money from his pocket and handed it to Papa. A long look passed between them.

Suddenly Kate remembered Anders' pig, Rosie. "What happened? Did you get a ribbon?"

Anders' eyes looked proud. "Sure did. A *blue* ribbon and something even better!"

Kate was curious. "What's that?"

A wide grin split his tanned face. "A man bought her. Gave a really good price!"

Kate felt his excitement. "And you're going to get your horse?"

"Nope. Not yet."

"Then a calf you can raise and sell for a horse?"

Something flickered in Anders' blue eyes, but it passed so quickly Kate thought she imagined it.

"Nope," he said. "But come on. I'll show you a mare I found. It'd be a good one."

Leaving Papa behind, Kate and Anders headed down the street. Soon they came to a place where horses were sold. Anders stopped. "See her? Isn't she a beauty?"

Before Kate stood a black horse tied to a tree. Her coat was shiny, her legs long and slender. The mare tossed her head, and Kate knew she was the spirited kind of horse Anders wanted.

"What's her name?"

When Anders didn't answer, Kate asked again.

"I'd call her Wildfire," he said, his voice low.

"I bet she'd go like wildfire. How much?"

"Little more than I got for the pig."

"Really? Not more than that? How come? She looks like a great horse."

"She is. Except for one thing." Anders walked around to the front of the mare.

As he stood silent and waiting, Kate followed. She looked, then quickly looked away. Across the mare's chest was a deep cut that was still healing.

Kate saw the pain in Anders' eyes. Pain she guessed was for the horse. "What happened?"

"Must have run into a fence. Lot of horses aren't used to barbed wire. Looks like this one ran straight for it "

"What'll happen to her?" Kate asked, afraid to look again.

"If someone takes care of her, making sure the wound doesn't get infected—"

"You could do it!"

A shadow flickered across Anders' face. "Maybe. Maybe not. It's taking a chance. Can't tell for sure if the tendons have been hurt."

"Did you ask Papa?

Anders nodded, but didn't look at Kate. "He thinks the mare will be all right."

"Then why don't you get it?" she prodded.

Anders still watched the horse, and seemed not to hear.

"Take a risk!"

Anders shook his head.

"What are you, a *scaredy-cat*?"

Suddenly Anders turned to Kate, his eyes flashing with anger. Yet, for the first time since Kate had known him, he walked away instead of answering. Kate had to run to catch up.

When they found Papa Nordstrom, Kate waited until Anders moved on to talk with a friend. Then, feeling as though her heart was tearing away from her body, she spoke up. "Why don't you use the money from the honey? Why don't you use it to help Anders buy Wildfire?"

Papa looked surprised. "The mare? But you worked all summer to save for an organ!"

"Yah." Kate seldom used the Swedish yes. But this time it said what she felt. "That horse—" Remembering the wound, she broke off, unable to explain that Wildfire needed Anders, and Anders needed the mare. "Who owns it?" she asked, not knowing what else to say.

"A man just outside Grantsburg," answered Papa. To Kate's disappointment, he changed the subject. "Let's go find Mama. It's time for a picnic. If we hurry, we won't keep her waiting."

Turning away, Papa bumped into another man. "Oh, excuse me!"

As the man lifted his hat, Kate saw his light brown hair, parted down the center. Dressed in a fine suit, he seemed out of place at the fair. He also seemed familiar.

"Don't I know you?" asked Papa, echoing Kate's thoughts.

"Eberly," answered the man, lifting his hat again. "Fred Eberly."

"Yah, sure," said Papa. "The salesman. Met you on the Blueberry Special last spring. Back in town again, I see."

"Right, right," said Eberly, his voice hearty. "Showing the merchants my new line for winter." He smiled, but somehow it didn't reach his eyes.

Kate shivered. For some reason she felt cold. Had a cloud passed over the sun? She glanced up, but the sun still sparkled in the crisp air.

Yet Kate couldn't shake off the feeling. Something bothered her. Was it the man's eyes? Their gray depths seemed stormy, as though he was angry, or mean. Kate couldn't explain it to herself. She only knew she didn't like Mr. Eberly.

Lifting his hat once more, Mr. Eberly moved away and disappeared in the crowd.

18

The Syrup Pail

*W*e saw Big Gust!" said Tina as all of them climbed into the wagon for the trip home.

"Do you know what he did?" Among his freckles Lars's blue eyes sparkled. "He picked up two troublemakers at the same time!"

Kate was curious. "Picked them up?"

"He held one guy under one arm and another guy under the other. And he carried them off to jail!"

Lars raised his right hand, promising he told the truth. With what she already knew about Big Gust, Kate didn't find it hard to believe. Yet she was silent most of the way home.

Before leaving Grantsburg, she had walked back to see the organ once more. It was gone, and so was the owner. Disappointment ripped through her, turning like a knife, sharp and awful.

Anders was also quiet. Kate wondered if he was thinking about Wildfire.

Most of all, she felt let down. *It was awful telling Papa to use that money for the mare. But what's worse—even though I offered, he didn't do it. Anders doesn't have a horse, and I don't have an organ.*

For Kate the pain went deep. *We both worked hard. Neither of us got what we worked for.* It seemed the whole world had turned dark.

Sunday morning dawned bright and crisp. Kate woke early to see mist rising above Rice Lake. For a moment the mist of tears dimmed her vision. She still felt upset about yesterday.

Trying to leave her discouragement behind, she put on her Sunday dress, then her locket. As she brushed her hair, Kate leaned toward the mirror for a better look at the treasured piece of jewelry.

Whenever she wore the locket, she felt warm inside, remembering Daddy. Kate hoped she would never forget her last birthday before he died. "Oh, Brendan!" Mama had said. "She's too young for such a fine gift."

Daddy had shook his head. His blue eyes danced as he grinned at Kate. "I've had good work this year. I want her to have it."

As though it were yesterday, Kate remembered how she felt when she received the heart-shaped locket. With a small hinge, it opened to a tiny picture of Mama on one side, Daddy on the other.

Thinking about that day, Kate could almost feel Daddy lifting her high in the air. She could almost hear his laughter and his Irish tenor voice singing the songs she loved. "She'll take good care of it," he told Mama. And Kate had. In all this time she had.

After Sunday dinner, Mama and Papa Nordstrom left to check on a sick neighbor. Lars and Tina went along. "If we don't get back, do the chores," Papa told Kate and Anders. "It means they need our help. I might have to go for the doctor."

As Kate cleaned up after the meal, she took the milk to the well. Being careful of her best dress, she lifted the trapdoor and lay down on her stomach to put the milk inside.

The splinter near the opening seemed longer. Carefully, Kate leaned over the jagged edge to reach under the boards covering the well. Hooking the rope onto the pail, she lowered the milk to the waterline.

Just then something nudged her back. Jerking with surprise, Kate scrambled to her knees. A cold nose touched her arm. "Lutfisk!"

The dog edged closer, waiting for Kate to scratch behind his ears. But suddenly she realized something. "My locket! It's gone!"

Feeling sick all over, Kate remembered her sudden jerk. Something had caught on the sharp end of the splinter. Had the locket fallen into the well?

Bending over, she looked down into the dark pit. Black water glimmered back at her. Daddy's gift!

Fear creeping into her heart, Kate sat back on her heels to think. The more she thought about it, the more impossible it became. Where else could the locket be? It had to be in the well!

"She'll take good care of the locket," Daddy had told Mama.

"But I haven't! I've lost it!" Kate cried out. "I've lost it!"

"What have you lost?" asked Anders, coming up behind her.

"My locket. My locket from Daddy. It's down in the well! What'll I do?"

Anders knelt at the trapdoor. "You're sure?"

Despair filling her voice, Kate told about Lutfisk. About the splinter and the sudden jerk. "I don't know where else it could be."

"Then let's do something about it."

"Do something? It's *gone!*" Kate wailed.

"Be quiet. Let me think."

"Are you crazy? What will thinking do? It's down the *well!*" Anders shushed her. "Stop acting like a woman."

"I *am* a woman. Well, almost."

For a long minute Anders knelt there, still looking down in the well. "I think it'll work."

"What will work?" Kate was afraid to hope. "Doesn't the water go way down to China?"

"Just do what I tell you," Anders ordered, his voice impatient. "First of all, take out the milk. Put it in the spring below the hill."

While Kate brought up the milk, Anders disappeared. When he returned, he wore old clothes and carried a ladder and a bucket on a rope. Without another word he tied the rope to the pipe above the platform and started bailing water from the well.

"But that's hopeless," said Kate. "If you take some water out, more will come in."

"Nope." Anders shook his head and kept bailing. "See this pump? Papa and I put it in last summer."

"So?"

"So the pipe going down in the well has a small hole below the frost line. When we pump the handle, water comes up through the pipe. When we stop pumping, the water we don't use drains back out through the hole. That way the pipe doesn't freeze in winter."

"And that's the water I see?"

"Yup! The water that drains out."

Kate wasn't sure she understood, but for two hours she and Anders took turns bailing water. At last the bucket scraped gravel.

"Great!" exclaimed Anders. "We're getting there."

Keeping on, they bailed out as much water as they could. Then the bucket seemed to hit something—something that wasn't the pipe. Anders stopped bailing and peered into the well.

"What is it?" Kate's voice sounded cross. She wanted to find the locket.

"I'm not sure," said Anders slowly. "Looks like a rock. But there wasn't a rock last summer."

They kept bailing, working around whatever it was. Finally Anders set the bucket on the grass next to the pump. Kate helped him lift the ladder through the trapdoor. Slowly they lowered the ladder until they felt the crunch of gravel.

"It's just long enough!" said Kate.

"I know. We had to use it last summer."

It was a tight fit, but Anders slipped through the trapdoor and down the ladder.

"Hey, Kate!" he yelled from the bottom, his voice sounding hollow.

Kate's heart jumped. "Did you find it?"

"Nope, but send down the bucket."

As soon as Anders had the bucket in his hands, he set something inside. "Haul it up!" he called.

Hand over hand Kate pulled up the bucket. "What's so heavy?"

As the bucket reached the light, she saw a syrup pail set inside. On the lid was the rock that held the pail under water. Knotted to the handle of the pail was a strong, thin rope. A rope dyed black.

A moment later, Anders called out again. "I found it!"

Soon he was out of the well, pulling himself back through the trapdoor. From his pocket he pulled Kate's locket and the broken chain.

Quick tears sprang into her eyes. "Anders, I can't believe it!"

"Believe it, believe it," he answered, his voice gruff with the sound that said, "Dumb girl!" But now Kate knew him well enough to recognize his teasing. As he handed her the locket, she felt she was getting buried treasure.

Drying it on her skirt, Kate held the jewelry up to the sun. "It's not even scratched."

"Are there pictures inside?"

With shaky fingers she opened the tiny clasp. On either side Mama and Daddy smiled up at her. Kate nodded, unable to speak.

Anders did it for her. "Good it was watertight."

For a moment neither of them spoke. To Kate it seemed impossible the locket and pictures were all right.

Anders broke the silence. "Well, seems like we've got us another treasure."

Kate looked up, wondering what he meant.

"The syrup pail. That's a strange rope." Going back to the pump, Anders knelt down, peering through the trapdoor. The top of the dark rope was secured to the far edge of the underside of the platform. "No wonder none of us saw it. I wonder how long it's been here?"

Returning to Kate, Anders lifted off the rock and wiped the outside of the pail dry. Then he took out his pocketknife. Prying one side, then another, he lifted the tight-fitting lid. "Take a look at this!"

Carefully they emptied the pail. First came glass beads like the ones they found under the stump.

"Lots of 'em," said Kate. "A jeweled comb . . ."

Coiling her long braid on top of her head, she pushed in the comb and fluttered her eyelashes like a fancy lady.

Anders wrinkled his nose. He was busy with the pail again. "Look!" he said, pulling out a pocketknife with a white bone handle.

Kate felt puzzled. "If someone is stealing, where does all this stuff come from?"

Anders was examining the pail. "Do you see the inside? Coated with candle wax. Even if the can leaked for some reason, the water wouldn't get through."

"Whoever it is—" Kate broke off, not wanting to finish the sentence.

"Is a hard customer. He's been thinking," said Anders.

At the bottom of the pail, Anders made the best find of all. "The copper piece!"

Kate picked it up from his hand. It was the same piece, all right. About four inches square and a quarter of an inch thick. Turning it over, she saw the word *Sverige* and the stamp of the crown of Sweden.

"We'll get a reward for sure!" Anders said.

"If we don't lose it again," Kate replied dryly.

Anders' eyes turned serious. "You're right. Let's pack it up and figure out what to do."

Refilling the syrup pail, they pressed down the lid and began talking in earnest.

"How about hiding it in the house?" asked Kate, thinking that would be safer.

"We never lock the doors. Don't know if we even have keys. Someone could walk in when we're out in the field working. Or in the barn milking the cows."

Back and forth they talked about the best place to hide something. With every idea they had, Anders wasn't satisfied.

"I know!" Kate exclaimed at last. "Look at this pail. What does it remind you of?"

"Our lunch buckets?"

"No, silly! Try again!"

Anders gave up.

"We used jars for the honey we sold, and had only two big tins for honey we kept. So we started filling extra syrup pails!"

Anders caught on. "And they're all in the root cellar! Let's go!"

Taking the pail, they set it on a shelf toward the back of the cellar. Alongside sat several pails of honey.

"Perfect!" said Anders. "If I didn't know it's the third one from the left, I'd never find it without opening every can. It even weighs almost the same."

Kate nodded. "But if you ever *need* to know, there's one clue. See this rust on the handle?" Kate picked up the pail, held it to the light, then set it down again. "It's the only pail with rust."

Carefully, Anders closed both doors of the root cellar.

"It's a real good hiding place," said Kate as she and Anders headed for the summer kitchen.

Just then, on the other side of the wagon track, the bushes moved.

Did someone touch them? For a moment Kate stood there watching. Finally she decided, *It's just the wind.*

Yet for some reason her uneasiness wouldn't go away.

19

Footsteps in the Night

$\mathcal{I}$'ll keep watch the first part of the night," said Anders. It was late, and Mama and Papa had not returned. One of Anders' bedroom windows overlooked the root cellar. "Remember our signal?"

Kate nodded. "When you knock on my wall, I'll take a turn at the storeroom window. But what do we do if the stranger comes?"

"We stay out of sight," said Anders. "We watch from a distance and try to get help."

Kate shivered. "Let's hope he doesn't come back tonight."

Anders agreed. He also decided to let Lutfisk stay outside. "Let's hope he doesn't find a skunk."

Before going to bed, Kate put on her old, dark work dress. Then, taking a needle and thread, she sewed a loop, bringing together the ends of the broken chain. Slipping the locket over her head, she tucked it inside her dress.

For a long time she lay awake. As Kate remembered the stranger in the woods, the terrors of her first day at Spirit Lake School returned. Trying to push those fears aside, she tossed and turned, then finally fell asleep.

Some time after midnight Kate woke to long, solid rapping

on her bedroom wall. Quietly she slipped out of bed and rapped back. Then she tiptoed to the storeroom.

In the dark she circled wooden boxes and bags of seed for next year's planting. When she reached the window, she found the view exactly what she needed. On all sides of the root cellar the yard was open. If the stranger came, Kate would be able to see him. Best of all, the full moon lit the entire area.

Kneeling down by the window, Kate soon lost track of time. A movement in the darkness made her wonder if she dozed. She rubbed her eyes and waited.

There it was again. Across the wagon track, between the granary and the chicken coop, the bushes parted. A shadow separated from the deeper shadow of the bushes. Slowly a dark figure emerged.

Without a sound it glided over the grass, then crossed the dirt track. For a moment it merged with the shadow of the summer kitchen, then moved on. Kate tensed, her heart climbing into her throat.

Silently the dark figure headed toward the root cellar. In the open space where the tree had fallen, the figure moved into the moonlight. The silhouette became a man with a beard, hat, and long hair.

Quickly Kate moved to the wall of Anders' room. Rap, she knocked. Pause. Rap, rap.

Stumbling through the darkness, she headed for the storeroom door. Once she fell over a box. Another time she tripped on a bag of grain, but caught herself. Finally she reached the hall and the door of Anders' room. There she knocked harder. Rap. Pause. Rap, rap.

No response. For a moment she waited, then pounded the signal again.

Turning, Kate slipped down the steps and out the front door. Crossing the porch, she remembered Lutfisk. Where was he? Why didn't he bark?

Running soundlessly on the grass, she hurried to the root cellar. Both doors stood partway open. Through the crack, Kate saw a lantern set on the dirt floor. Now and then the man moved closer to the light. It was the stranger, all right.

As Kate watched, he lifted one syrup pail after another, shaking them as though trying to decide which was his.

I'd better find Anders. Kate started edging backward. *Maybe he's staying out of sight. He'll keep a safe distance.*

Then, from somewhere beyond the barn, a horse whinnied. "I'll see what's there, then hide," Kate promised herself.

Soundlessly she crept beyond the root cellar. Staying on the grass, she started running, glad for the full moon. As she came around the far side of the barn, she found a team of horses and a wagon filled with crates.

Then Kate's heart did strange flip-flops. Toward the back of the wagon was a big wooden trunk. This time she felt sure it wasn't Mama's but one just like it.

In that moment all of Kate's scared feelings fell away. Only one thought remained. *What's in the trunk?*

As she climbed into the wagon, one of the horses moved slightly. The harness jangled.

Kate froze. Except for the breathing of the horses, the night air was silent. Working her way between the crates, Kate reached the trunk. A padlock hung on the clasp, but it was open!

Slipping the padlock out, Kate lifted the lid of the trunk. Yawning blackness met her. Was it empty? A pang of disappointment shot through her.

Then Kate pushed the lid farther back. Something reflected the light of the full moon. Reaching into the darkness, she felt a syrup pail like the one she and Anders found in the well.

As she picked it up, one of the horses snorted. Again Kate froze, listening. This time she heard a sound. Someone was coming! Was it the stranger?

Quickly she dropped the pail into the trunk, closed the lid, and replaced the padlock. *Where can I hide?* she wondered, filled with panic. No bushes nearby. Around the wagon, the land was clear.

Then Kate spied a large wooden crate, open at the top. Something dark lay at the bottom. Reaching down, she discovered a heavy horse blanket. Tumbling into the crate, she crawled beneath the blanket and pulled it over her head.

A moment later, Kate heard stealthy footsteps on the dirt track. Closer and closer they came. Kate huddled in the crate, scarcely breathing.

Someone climbed into the wagon and edged past the crate where Kate hid. Listening, she heard the lid of the trunk open, then close.

Once more, footsteps approached the crate. Kate's fingers clenched in a nervous ball as she held her breath. The footsteps passed by toward the front of the wagon.

The seat creaked as the person dropped on it and clucked the horses. The wagon started to move, slowly and quietly at first, then picking up speed.

Kate let out her breath. *Have I got myself in a fix!* For a moment longer she lay there, afraid to move. Then, not making a sound, she lifted the horse blanket and looked around.

Far above, bright stars lit the night sky. Under the full moon Kate saw the pine boards of the wooden crate that surrounded her. Straight ahead, in the side of the box facing front, a large knothole offered a place to see.

Kneeling inside the box, Kate pressed her face against the wood and squinted. Through the knothole she saw a man's back, a pulled-down hat, and long hair. It was the stranger, all right!

As he flicked the reins, the horses broke into a trot.

Where're we going? Kate's panic was gone now, but a scared feeling still gnawed at her stomach. Then she felt the wagon make a right turn. They were headed toward Grantsburg.

She wanted to stand up and look around. But what if the stranger looked back? After thinking a moment, Kate decided to memorize the turns.

Yet a wave of hopelessness washed over her. She tried to push away her frightening thoughts, but they kept returning.

Eleven miles to Grantsburg.

Eleven long miles.

Eleven miles filled with trees and bears and screech owls.

Eleven scary miles.

Kate had been to Grantsburg only twice—that day in March and on Saturday for the fair. Even to herself she didn't want to admit how quickly she could become lost. *Where's Anders, anyway? Lot of good our signal did!*

As the horses trotted along the road, Kate had another awful thought. *Did Anders hear my knock? If he didn't, no one will know I'm gone!*

With each passing minute Kate grew more afraid. Panic returned in spite of her efforts to push it aside. Now the crate seemed like a prison. *Maybe I can jump out.*

Then her mind took over. *We're going too fast. I'd get hurt for sure.*

Lying down in the crate, she tried to think. At first her ideas whirled, refusing to come in order. Yet she couldn't go anywhere. She had to figure something out. Gradually she settled down to some hard thinking.

The wagon creaked as the horses moved forward and the miles fell away. Huddled under the horse blanket, Kate felt glad for its warmth. She lay looking up, watching the stars. Her head hurt from trying to work out a plan.

They must have traveled over an hour when Kate felt the wagon turn a corner and stop. Quickly she pulled the blanket over her head. As she listened, the stranger climbed down.

After a moment Kate pushed aside the blanket and peered through the knothole. Only the horses were in sight. For a moment longer she waited, listening. When no sound came, she stood up in the crate.

In the light of the full moon Kate saw trees growing close on both sides of the road. The stranger must have slipped into the woods, but she could not tell in which direction.

As Kate looked around, she saw that the wagon stood near a crossroad. The horses waited just far enough ahead to show her where they'd been and where they were headed.

Are we still on the road to Grantsburg? She didn't know. One tree seemed the same as the next.

Like a squirrel running for cover, Kate's thoughts scurried this way and that. *What should I do? Get out? Hide behind a tree?*

The woods seemed even more frightening than the wagon. *I'd never find my way home. And which way did the stranger go? What if I met him coming back?*

Then she thought of something else. *The road's dry and wagon tracks hard to follow. How will Anders and Papa find me?*

Desperately Kate looked around for something to use— something that marked their trail. Something Anders and Papa would recognize, but the mysterious stranger wouldn't see.

Then she remembered her locket, still tucked inside her

dress. Climbing down from the wagon, she hurried to a bush a short distance after the turn in the road. Reaching up, Kate hung the necklace over a limb. *It's so small. Can Anders and Papa possibly see it?*

Just then a bloodcurdling screech split the night air. As the sound echoed in the stillness, Kate shuddered. Filled with panic, she headed for the wagon.

It did no good to tell herself it was a screech owl. Frantically, she pulled herself up.

As she tumbled into the wagon, Kate heard a branch snap in the woods. *The stranger! He's coming back!*

Desperate, Kate headed for the crate and stepped inside. As she reached for the blanket, she heard another sound, this time from the road. There it was again, soft and low. "Woof! Woof!"

Still standing in the crate, Kate turned in that direction. Near the corner where they'd turned was a low silhouette, dark in the moonlight. *Lutfisk!*

Kate wanted to hug the dog, to get down and follow him home. Yet as she started to climb out of the crate, she heard another branch crack in the woods. The sound was closer and Lutfisk too far away. In another moment the stranger would be here.

I'd never make it to cover! Kate's fear was back again.

Then she knew what to do. "Lutfisk!" she called in a hoarse whisper. The dog started toward her. "Go get Anders!"

The dog stopped. For a moment he waited, and Kate's throat tightened. Then she remembered the command Anders used, telling the dog to get cows. *But will Lutfisk obey ME?*

Raising her arm high, she motioned to the right, using Anders' command. Lutfisk still waited.

Again Kate raised her arm and motioned to the right. In the moonlight Lutfisk cocked his head as though torn about what to do. Then, seeming to make up his mind, he turned back the way he came, heading off at a steady lope.

Once the dog stopped and looked around. Then he disappeared in the darkness.

Kate dropped down in the crate. As she pulled the blanket over her shoulders, she heard footsteps on the dirt road. Quickly she covered her head.

The steps grew closer. Closer. Closer.

20

Race Against Time

*H*uddled under the horse blanket, Kate heard the man climb into the wagon. Once again he worked his way between the crates to the trunk at the back. Dropping something inside, he walked forward again.

"Giddyup!" he told the horses.

For Kate the miles seemed to last forever. The mysterious stranger seemed in no hurry to get wherever he was going. Though she tried hard, Kate could not keep track of the turns.

Whenever the stranger stopped the wagon, she listened until unable to hear footsteps. Then, standing up, she peered into the darkness.

Always one tree looked the same as the next. Always Kate looked for another chance to mark the way; it never came.

With each stop her despair deepened. "Anders, where are you?" She wanted to cry out. Then, "Will Lutfisk get help?" And then, "If I get out of this, will I ever find my locket again?"

In the night sky the moon hung low. A cool breeze sprang up. Shivering and tired, Kate pulled the blanket over her shoulders. As she lay curled in a ball, her panic grew. "I'm scared, God," she prayed. "Really scared."

Then the breeze touched her face, and Kate thought of something she hadn't really believed before. Something important.

"You took care of me that day with the bull, didn't you, God? You helped me when I was lost in the woods and when I was afraid in the cellar.

"When everything changes, and I'm scared of those changes, can I count on you, God? No matter what happens, you're the same, aren't you?"

Deep in her being, Kate knew something more. "When I'm scared, you're my biggest help. If I'd let you, you'd be with me all the time, wouldn't you? Even in this awful wilderness?"

As the breeze changed to a sharp wind, Kate pulled the blanket over her head. Each time her fear came back, she repeated the verse Papa and Anders read: "God *is* our refuge and strength, a very present help in trouble." Before long, she changed the words into a prayer. "God is *my* refuge and strength, *my* help in trouble."

And then, Kate was asleep.

———

When she wakened, the wagon had stopped. Kate felt confused. *Where am I?* Then she remembered and became wide awake. Fear tightened her stomach. *What happened to Anders? Where's the stranger?*

As she pushed the blanket aside, light shone into the crate. To Kate's surprise she found the sun high in the sky, high enough to be edging toward noon. She felt even more surprised that she could sleep at a time like this.

With the blanket still covering her back, she raised up enough to see through the knothole. The wagon seat was empty. Beyond, the horses stood still, as though tied to a rail.

Then Kate remembered the trunk. She hadn't seen what the stranger put into it, but she had no doubt what was there—syrup pails filled with whatever the stranger had stolen. Kate tried to work it out, knowing the man must have hidden pails along a route and waited with collecting them until he thought it was safe.

Just then she heard voices. "Over here," called a man, and Kate jerked the blanket back over her head. Another man answered, and the two kept talking as they moved closer to the wagon.

"I know one of those voices," Kate told herself. "Who is it?"

Closing her eyes, she concentrated. As hard as she tried, she couldn't figure it out. She couldn't connect the voice with a face.

Then Kate heard someone at the back of the wagon, lifting out the end board. Fear shot through her.

Wood scraped against wood. "One, two, heave!" called the familiar voice. Something heavy dropped onto something else.

Kate followed the sounds in her thoughts. *There goes the trunk. Where's he taking it?*

From the back of the wagon came more scraping. Then the wagon jiggled as someone climbed in and started shoving crates around.

Kate's fingers clenched into nervous fists. *What if they pick up this crate? They'd find me for sure!*

Close beside the crate in which Kate lay motionless, the familiar voice spoke. "That's the last one. All right if I leave your horses here?"

"Move 'em over a bit, out of the way," called the other voice. "I'll take 'em back to the livery later."

"Your horse blanket's here," said the man near Kate. "Want it now?"

"Nah, leave it for the next customer."

As Kate listened, a wagon rolled away. Beside her, footsteps moved forward. Someone clucked the horses, and they backed away from the rail.

Slowly Kate raised up, pressing her face against the knothole. Surprise rippled through her.

Instead of long black hair and a crumpled hat, the driver's short brown hair showed beneath a spotless hat. Instead of a wrinkled black coat with a tear in one sleeve, the man wore a well-pressed suit coat.

Kate felt confused. *What happened to the mysterious stranger?*

She struggled to think. *There's something about this man—something that bothers me. Something I should know.*

As Kate watched through the knothole, the man stopped the

wagon. Jumping down, he tied the horses to a rail and hurried off, still within Kate's line of vision. *His shoulders. There's something about his shoulders.*

A moment later the man stepped onto a wooden platform, and his shoes clicked.

Then Kate knew. She gasped as all the pieces fell into place.

In the distance a train whistle blew. Again it sounded, closer this time. Kate heard the hiss of brakes, the squeal of iron on iron. The Blueberry Special!

"They'll turn the engine around," she muttered. "They'll fill it up with water. Maybe they'll need coal. But then they'll leave."

The scared feeling was back in her stomach. "Once the train leaves Grantsburg, that trunk will be gone. All those stolen things lost forever!"

Around Kate, the noise increased. Men called to each other, and Kate felt sure they were turning the engine.

Then the stranger moved out of range of her knothole view. "I'll climb out. I'll run for help."

Pushing back the blanket, she took one last look through the knothole. The stranger was back, looking straight toward the wagon.

Once more Kate crouched down. *What'll I do? The train will leave. He'll get away!*

Her frantic thoughts raced on. *I'll stand up. I'll walk right up to him!*

Even as the thought came, she knew it wouldn't work. *It's my word against his. No one will believe me!*

Then a wagon pulled alongside the one in which Kate huddled. Someone whistled, and Kate recognized it. Anders whistling to Lutfisk!

Relief poured through her. The next second she felt scared again. *How can I warn him? He'll look right at the stranger and not recognize him.*

Then Kate remembered the signal she and Anders had worked out. Rap. Pause. Rap, rap, she knocked against the wooden crate.

Once again she rapped, harder this time. Rap. Pause. Rap, rap. A moment later, Kate heard Anders' voice.

"Kate?" he asked softly from alongside the wagon.

Kate wanted to shout. Instead, she, too, spoke quietly. "Anders? The mysterious stranger is the man standing right in front of you."

"The one with the hat and suit?"

"In a minute he'll get on the train and be gone."

"But this wagon? He'll just leave it?"

"He must have rented it at the livery stable."

"And he took the stuff? How do you know?"

"It's in his trunk." Kate was growing impatient. "You have to get help! If I stand up, he'll see me. He'll know I followed him."

Anders took only a second to decide. "Stay right where you are. I'll get Big Gust."

"You know where he lives?"

"A couple blocks from here. In the fire station."

The silence stretched long, then a wagon creaked from somewhere near the train. Soon they would put the trunk in the baggage car. "Come on, Anders, hurry up!" she wanted to shout.

Through the knothole, she watched trainmen pull up the long spout of the water tank. "All ah-boooooard! All ah-boooooard!" called the conductor.

The neatly dressed man turned his back toward Kate, falling into line with the other passengers.

Standing up in the crate, Kate scrambled out of the wagon, determined to stop him. As she reached the ground, Mama and Papa Nordstrom came down the street.

"Kate!" Mama exclaimed. "We've been looking for you. Anders came to the neighbors and told us you were missing. Where have you been?"

"Mama! Just a minute! We have to stop him!"

"Stop who?" asked Mr. Nordstrom.

"Mr. Eberly! He's a thief!"

"A thief!"

"Anders will tell you!"

Just then Big Gust hurried up. Anders and Lutfisk ran alongside to keep pace with the marshal's long strides.

"A thief, Papa," said Anders. "We've got to stop him!"

Big Gust looked at Mr. Nordstrom. "Are they telling the truth?"

"I don't know," said Papa. "But they've told the truth up 'til now."

Big Gust scratched his head. "It's serious business, stopping someone."

"If you could see inside his trunk—" Kate interrupted.

"His trunk?"

"The big wooden one. The one they're loading right now," she said. "The things he stole are in there, in syrup pails. See how heavy it is?"

As they watched, two men struggled with lifting the trunk onto the train. "Come on, Gust, give us a hand," one of them called.

As Big Gust started over, a leather handle broke. The trunk crashed to the ground. One of the corners split open. Through the opening, Kate saw the shiny metal of a syrup pail.

"Pull it aside, away from the train," ordered Big Gust.

He turned to Kate. "Now, young lady, you'll have to show me the owner of this trunk."

Soon Big Gust had Mr. Eberly off the train. As Mr. Eberly came down the metal steps, his shoes clicked.

"Miner's shoes!" exclaimed Anders in a low voice. "He must have worked in a mine, somewhere away from here."

"In March his face was too white," said Kate. "As if he didn't get much sun. He's the man in the woods, all right. He wore a wig and false beard."

As Kate and Anders moved closer, Big Gust spoke to Mr. Eberly. "The men dropped the trunk. I want you to check that everything's all right."

"Oh, I'm sure it is," answered Mr. Eberly. His voice sounded calm, but his eyes looked nervous.

Big Gust insisted. "Don't want you to have trouble later. Unlock the trunk."

"But I'll miss my train."

"The train will wait, and so will I." Big Gust's voice was firm and as polite as always. Yet as he towered above Mr. Eberly, the marshal's face no longer looked kind.

Slowly Mr. Eberly unlocked the trunk.

"Hmmmmmm. What have we got here?" asked Big Gust, his face innocent. "Maybe you better open one of these pails for me."

Kate hurried forward. "I'll show you which one," she said.

Mr. Eberly turned to her, an angry flush on his face, his gray eyes stormy. "Who are you? This is my business, not yours."

"Well, then," said Big Gust, "no harm in doing what she asks. What do you have in mind, young lady?"

Quickly, before anyone could stop her, Kate unloaded the trunk, setting one syrup pail after another on the ground. Near the bottom, she found what she wanted—the pail with rust on the handle.

"I'll tell you what's in this one," she said. "A copper piece with a stamp of Sweden!"

Suddenly Mr. Eberly bolted. Big Gust barely moved. Reaching out one long arm, he grabbed hold of the back of Eberly's collar. For a moment the village marshal swung the man off the ground. Then, as if in slow motion, Big Gust set Eberly down on the platform.

The smaller man did not move.

Then the marshal called over a drayman with his horses and wagon. Refilling the trunk, Big Gust picked it up and loaded it onto the wagon.

Kate couldn't believe it. "All by himself!"

Anders laughed. Papa turned to Mama, a grin on his face.

Big Gust acted as though nothing out of the ordinary had happened. "I'll take this man to jail and be right back."

Brushing against Kate's skirt for attention, Lutfisk wouldn't be ignored any longer. As she hugged her thanks, he licked Kate's face and woofed.

Then Mama's arms went around her. "I'm *proud* of you, Kate!" she exclaimed, though concern still showed in her face.

When Mr. Nordstrom hugged her too, Kate guessed how afraid he'd been. "Swedes don't hug in public," she wanted to say. Instead, she pulled back and looked into his eyes. "It's awfully good to see you, Papa."

A flash of surprise crossed Mr. Nordstrom's face, then was

gone. "It's awfully good to see *you*, Kate," he echoed, his voice gruff.

When Kate turned to Anders, he looked embarrassed. "Did you rap on my door? I never heard you. I must have just fallen asleep."

Then he told what happened. "Just as I finished milking, Lutfisk found me in the barn. He barked until I followed him to your window. That's how I knew you were gone."

Papa took up the story. "Anders walked as fast as he could to find us at the neighbors. We hitched up the horses."

"Lutfisk ran ahead," Anders told her. "When we came to a crossroads, he took the turn, still sniffing. He sniffed his way over to your locket, where it hung on a branch."

"It reflected the morning sun," Mama added, handing the locket to Kate. "At first we wondered . . ." Her eyes glistened with tears. "Then we decided you hung it there to show us where to go."

Kate nodded. "And the mystery's solved!" Turning to Anders, she explained about Mr. Eberly. "Remember how you wondered why the stranger kept disappearing? He's a salesman who comes to town now and then to show his wares—for spring, summer, fall, and winter! He brought a large trunk, filled with samples."

"And if he decided to sell his samples, he filled it up with whatever he stole!" guessed Anders.

"Remember your trunk, Mama?" Kate asked. "He must have gotten extra greedy. I wonder if he would have taken what he wanted, then sent the trunk back to the depot, saying it wasn't his?"

"So!" said Papa as Big Gust returned. "Let's celebrate!"

"Celebrate?" asked Kate. But no one would let her in on the secret.

When they reached Big Gust's rooms in the fire station, Anders walked over to something big sitting in the middle of the floor. It was covered with a large cloth, which Anders pulled off with a flourish.

There stood the organ Kate had seen at the fair. In the sunlight streaming through a window, the oak wood gleamed gold. Before the keyboard sat an organ stool as though waiting for someone to sit down to play.

"It's for you, Kate," Papa said quietly.

Kate stood there, unable to speak.

"Were the bee stings worth it?" he asked.

Kate nodded, still unable to speak.

"We brought it here on Saturday. Big Gust was going to bring it out today. We wanted to surprise you."

Kate found her voice. "But the money? I wanted Anders to get the mare."

Anders returned her look, but did not speak.

"He figured you needed the organ more," said Papa, his voice soft. "With the money from his pig and the honey you sold, plus what was left over from your mama selling furniture, we had just the amount we needed."

Once Kate would have taken whatever she could get. Now she felt strange receiving such a gift.

"Anders wants a horse?" Big Gust broke in. "Boys your age don't own a horse! You're sure you're old enough?"

Big Gust winked at Papa, then turned back to Anders. "Do you have one picked out?"

Anders told the big Swede about Wildfire. "If she's okay."

"She will be," said Papa. "She'll always have a scar across her chest, but it won't hurt her running. Because of it, she won't cost as much."

Big Gust's smile stretched from one side of his face to the other. "Well, I have just the thing for you, Anders. That is, if you and Kate can agree on what to do. Trader Carlson posted a reward when he lost his copper piece from Sweden. It might be just what you need for that horse."

"What about it, Kate?" asked Papa. "It's up to you."

Anders looked at Kate, a question in his eyes, a question he seemed unable to ask.

As Kate nodded, her excitement spilled over just thinking about all they could do with both an organ and a horse.

Anders leaped into the air, his arms high above his head. "I can't believe it!"

Kate grinned. "Believe it, believe it!" she teased, remembering how Anders rescued her locket from the well.

But she kept another thought to herself. *Maybe the Wisconsin wilderness isn't so bad after all! I wonder what will happen next?*

Acknowledgments

My thanks to the countless individuals who answered my questions and helped shape the lives of Kate and Anders. I'm especially grateful to those who spent long hours telling me the way it was:

Phillip Johnson and Carl Lindell, Sr. talked about the Minneapolis of long ago. From Wade Brask came Anders' dog Lutfisk, the school bell, and the root cellar. The house, barn, and summer kitchen belong to Emma Bergstrom Haight. Arnold Johnson remembered his boyhood in a country school. Helen Tyberg knew what it meant to be both a student and a teacher. John and Gladys Olson recalled the Blueberry Special and salesmen coming to town. Gunhild Kempe talked about growing up on a farm. Mildred Hedlund checked my tales of Big Gust.

Maurice Crownhart and the Grantsburg Centennial Committee provided both pictures and history in *Strolling Through a Century*. Through conversation and her book, *Pieces of the Past*, Eunice Kanne offered her own careful research and a wide variety of details, including Trader Carlson's copper piece.

Walter and Ella Johnson deserve special mention for reading the manuscript, and for sharing ideas about Kate's locket, the well, and the use of dynamite and sadirons.

As we talked together, I came to know all of these people.

They helped me dream about what it was like to be a child in times past.

My gratitude also to Charette Barta, Ron Klug, Jerry Foley, Penelope Stokes, Terry White, and my husband Roy for their work on the manuscript and their ongoing encouragement.

A Note From Lois

Thanks to each of you who have written to tell me how much you like the ADVENTURES OF THE NORTHWOODS and THE RIVERBOAT ADVENTURES. I enjoy hearing from my readers and feel as though we've become friends through books.

If you would like to receive my newsletter, let me know by writing to:

> Lois Walfrid Johnson
> Bethany House Publishers
> 11300 Hampshire Ave. S.
> Minneapolis, MN 55438

Please include a *stamp* on an *envelope addressed to yourself* for *each* letter you request.